Mean Grey Old Morning

William R. Burkett, Jr.

"These short stories are
as good as it gets.'

- Shirrel Rhoades
Former Fiction Editor
The Saturday Evening Post

Mean
Grey Old
Morning

Mean Grey Old Morning

William R. Burkett, Jr.

**The New
Atlantian Library**

The New Atlantian Library is an imprint of
ABSOLUTELY AMAZING eBOOKS

Published by Whiz Bang LLC, 926 Truman Avenue, Key West, Florida 33040, USA

For information contact:
Publisher@AbsolutelyAmazingEbooks.com

ISBN-13: 978-0692411780 (New Atlantian Library, The)
ISBN-10: 069241178X

Kinsella created the term "Brautigans" for short, eclectic pieces of writing, and studying Richard Brautigan inspired me to try it for myself, so this is dedicated to Brautigan and to the creator of "Shoeless Joe," my favorite baseball book ...

1

Mean Grey Old Morning

Mean grey old morning.

Immolation of someone else's diary was not how I had planned to start my day.

It was early March of 1974. I had been out of gainful employment since the previous June, trying to write fiction and babysit my infant son. My wife worked as a secretary, driving back and forth to Tacoma in a $40 Pontiac Grand Prix that would be worth a small fortune now. Nobody wanted the big Detroit iron that year. The Arabs had supposedly squeezed off the world's supply of cheap oil, and you waited in long lines at gas stations and hoped they'd let you have five gallons, if any was left when it was your turn.

It wasn't the first winter I spent in the Pacific Northwest. It wouldn't be the last. But it was one of the toughest. I first saw Washington State in summer and watched June blend into July amid squalls of rain and dismal temperatures. By the spring of 1974, I had the uneasy feeling that I was living in the bottom of an uncleaned aquarium.

It was a mean grey old morning. I didn't know then that was what to call it.

I wanted some warmth in the house, so I touched off a milk carton and some twisted newspaper pages in the fireplace, trying to get the split alder wood to ignite, and knock the damp chill off. The baby was still restive, after a restless night; the chimney wasn't drawing yet; I needed more paper. There was a brown grocery sack beside the firewood carrier. Inside were hundreds of pages ripped from a bound diary, all jumbled together. The earliest entries I noticed were for 1936.

My wife said a friend of theirs, a remarkable, gravel-voiced Texas lady who was a radic-libber before anyone coined the term, was preparing to die. She wasn't particularly ill right then, just clearing the decks and settling accounts, so to speak.

The diary was her mother's.

She could not bring herself to burn it. But she had decreed that burn it must.

The thought of consigning the written harvest of a life to the flames made me vaguely ill. Still, it was her wish and the fire was foundering. So I began the immolation.

I held my curiosity down by main force, lest I spend the whole day in a dank room, trespassing in someone else's memories. I couldn't suppress a yearning wonder if some eternal truth might not be crisping into ash and smoke, borne away on the weak blue-grey plume the chimney finally produced. The alder began to crackle greedily. I fed the flames more words, more emotion, more vivid recollections. My eye fell on the top sheet of a new handful.

"Another mean grey old morning to contend with..."

Just a glimpse of that phrase, as my hand completed the already-begun gesture.

The fire fattened and belched, and almost began to purr. I fixed a Thermos of hot tea for my wife's drive to work, and backed the Pontiac out of the boggy, treacherous driveway. She thought she might be able to find gas for the beast today.

I was slower to feed the fire then.

Words floated by my gaze. In San Francisco, one day in 1944, the diarist visited a lonely friend for dinner. She saw the residential lights running down along the bay there as "a necklace of brilliants" against the night and fog. There was one funeral attendance. There were probably more; as one grows older, it becomes a usual thing. There was a fondly recalled trip to Berkeley, California. Each Sunday church visit was dutifully recorded.

But not once, as far as I could determine, for worship.

She went to church to "lobby." Frequently the word was in quotes; but she never explained why. How enigmatic. How charming. The Greek demand for outer logic and precise definition be damned. A host of possibilities unfolded themselves as the diary died. I wrote down one in my own journal:

"Lobby: A cynic's evaluation of the power of prayer?"

The fire was so hearty now it sucked the marrow from the pages and spit twisted bits of carbon up the chimney. I fed it faster, and it gurgled with surfeit. The room was warm, the baby content, and I was just finishing my grim work. The remaining pages of the diary, with its bulk already consumed, seemed drained of their vitality, sentenced to die, awaiting the flames. An unrelenting toll of repetitious early risings on dreary mornings, but how the day often turned "lovely" later on.

Almost the last to burn was Jim, a brief flare of renewed passion.

An anniversary of an old grief was commemorated. It dawned clear and bright, and the diarist noted the irony. Jim was either the love of her lifetime – or a Beagle hound. Once more, the charm of blurred distinctions. But the emanation of pain from the words was tangible. Then the words were gone, like Jim.

The baby was asleep, his head propped on the belly of my patient Labrador retriever. I sat for a long time, gazing out the window at the chimney smoke adrift in the windless, dripping gloom. Someone once said you can spend your whole life putting words on paper and be lucky to find one phrase that resonates.

Mean grey old morning.

2

Sudden Death on Merry Street

Call it the summer or early fall of 1946. Not really ancient history, not quite.

We still called our refrigerator an "icebox." It had even been built to look like one, before post-war designers got hold of kitchen appliances. Actual ice still was a principal method of cooling for small neighborhood grocery stores in the South.

Horse-drawn wagons still made the morning rounds, hauling block-ice for the walk-in coolers of the grocery stores. The arrival of the ice wagon was a daily ritual of my youngest memory, fresh as yesterday, etched on some of those organic chips of memory which now crowd my brain with an infinity of random moments. I was three going on four that year...

The varnished red spokes of the high wagon wheels glisten as they spin in the already-hot Georgia morning sun. The big green ice wagon, drawn by four clopping white horses, big as Percherons in my mind's eye, rumbles to the curb in front of McMichael's Grocery, across Walton Way. Bald Mr. Mac, broad-shouldered and big-bellied in his crisp white open-necked shirt, swathed in his customary ankle-length butcher's apron with the strings tied in front, props open his front door with a wooden milk crate. Sunlight flashes from his thick horn-rimmed glasses.

The two icemen go right to work. They drop the tailgate and untie and slide the stiff brown canvas tarp up the wagon toward the front. One of them climbs in with huge rust-red ice tongs. He begins to slide glistening fifty-pound blocks of ice out from under the tarp and toward the tailgate. Before the first block can tip off into the street, the second man tongs it neatly, turning in one fluid motion to carry it inside. Mr. Mac has his own tongs, and steps up to catch the second block. His motions are slower and more deliberate, without the consummate grace of the iceman.

The slender iceman and the burly grocer strike up a simple effective rhythm, as the man in the box feeds them the big ice blocks. The wagon bed is insulated with fresh sawdust, richly resinous in the early heat. The passage of the blocks of ice across the sawdust makes a shush...shush sound in the still morning. Very little car traffic this time of day. When the delivery is done, the icemen retie the tarp, remount the high sprung seat. The driver wheels the team smartly in a U-turn in front of McMichael's across the broad expanse of the street, and then lines them out down Merry Street right past our back porch. The loud clop of hooves on pavement is muffled in the red dirt of unpaved Merry Street, a shady green tunnel of huge maples that cuts the stifling heat, even at midday.

Sixteen big hooves and those twinkling wheels raise a

pall of red Georgia dust. I know, sort of, that Merry Street eventually leads to Central Avenue, which grownups say runs parallel to Walton Way over there somewhere.

Over there is where the icehouse is, and Colonial Bakery, where my mother works and brings home aromatic miniature loaves for me, baked from the day's leftovers. I was amazed on my first trip to Central Avenue in my grandfather's 1937 Plymouth by the unbelievable Lily Tulip Cup plant, whose main entrance is shaped like a giant white paper cup, several stories tall, with the trademark design painted just beneath the rolled lip.

All is peaceful in this random memory, all as usual on so many of those distant mornings.

Until this next moment:

A tiny yapping dog escapes its yard across Merry Street, barking furiously. It fearlessly rushes beneath the hooves of the wheel horses, startling them. They half-rear and lurch into the lead team.

All four horses suddenly begin to run. The red dust explodes and boils across our back yard. Our old screen porch trembles with the sudden thunder of their hooves. The icemen shout angrily, the driver's whip cracks, everything is in sudden, frantic motion...

The dog dodges back from flailing pie-plate hooves.

Whap...whap. Sharp as the driver's whip. The yap instantly silenced.

Front wheel, rear wheel, thumping over something in the dust, then a small broken bundle of fur tumbling to the side of the street.

At the end of the block, the driver standing and leaning back against the reins, the team slows to a ponderous jog, then a walk. But the wagon doesn't stop. Doesn't come back. The motionless little dusty lump lies unnoticed in the gutter.

The processional of memory is always the same.

The peace of the morning, the momentary panic, the noise and explosion of red dust and the shouting, the porch shaking. Then the small dusty bundle of stillness. And the team methodically clopping away into the distance.

There was no wiser head awake that morning to put sudden death into perspective. I don't remember ever telling a grownup about it. I doubt I would have had the words, at that age. We moved away from there just after I completed my first decade of existence, and the subject never came up.

Now, almost half a million hours later – and an infinity of moments – I still carry with me that first vivid unsettling realization that death can come out of nowhere on a serene morning that is just like any other. And the ice wagon of our destruction will go right on about its business, departing at a methodical clop into the tunnel of its own oblivion.

3

Mourning for the Crossroads

When I was a very young boy I understood pretty early that my grandmother spoke the language differently than other people. She was a born storyteller and her language evoked vivid images in my impressionable brain. One of the most vivid was when we heard a far-off train whistle in the night and she would intone: "The frogs lowered their croaking in the millpond and in the distance the midnight freight mourned for the crossroads."

It was understood without discussion that this sentence was rich with meaning. It was years before I knew that the lines were the opening of a never-published novel that she had written as a teenager, and then burned when her mother refused her permission to accept an offer of purchase from a newspaper syndicate. Writers were no better than harlots by my great grandmother's lights.

I knew what "moan" meant, though, and those distant train whistles sounded like they were in pain to me. At age nine, in keeping with the traditions of the Old South, I already had taken part in the solemnity of funerals and witnessed firsthand the formal, waxy stillness of the recently dead laid out in their coffins. So I knew what mourning was, too. The bereaved sometimes made sounds a little like those midnight freights out past East Boundary. The words confused themselves in my young brain.

Trains off across there somewhere had mourned for the crossroads my entire short life. I was sure they always would, an unchanging symbol of all that was distant and mysterious, and sometimes hurtful, in the world.

My unquestioning certainty changed in a single moment out on the Savannah River levee.

My grandfather was always taking my brother and me shooting out on levee. We would set up tin cans and empty whiskey bottles in the waste ground between the levee and the river, and then stand up on the levee and shoot down. My grandfather said this was to prevent dangerous ricochets by the little .22 bullets. Every one of those colorful little pasteboard boxes containing fifty .22 Long Rifle shells had a printed warning on the flap: "Range one mile – Be Careful!" We always were. My grandfather was fierce about ricochets.

One day we were shooting on the levee, near where the train tracks crossed it on the way to the river trestle into South Carolina. My brother was six that year, finally big enough that my grandfather didn't have to help him hold his little Remington single-shot bolt action. He was getting to be a good shot fast, totally focused on the sights. I cradled my Marlin repeater in the crook of my arm and stared hard at the bottles to see where his shots hit.

Something went BLAT-T-T-T-TTTT behind me so loud I almost dropped my rifle.

I spun around and here came this huge silver streamlined monster of a locomotive rushing toward the levee crossing, pulling a long line of passenger cars. They still had long passenger trains then.

There was no smokestack, no steam.

"Wave," my grandfather said.

He took off the blue mattress-ticking engineer's hat that he always wore outdoors and waved at the silver monster. Earl waved. I waved. The guy leaning out of the high side window of the locomotive, looking small as a toy soldier way up there, tugged off his own engineer's cap and waved back.

The train horn went BLAT-T-T-T again. No mournful whistle.

Then the silver monster was gone, sweeping on toward the river, that harsh sound trailing away strangely. At that age I had no idea what a Doppler effect was. The passenger cars flashed by, blink-quick glimpses of people in the windows, as the rumble click-click of the steel wheels washed over us with the rush of air from the train's passage. The horn sounded again off across there, probably when the locomotive hit the trestle.

I didn't realize I was staring after the train long after it was gone until my grandfather said something I didn't hear.

"What was that?" I said, meaning the locomotive. "What made that sound?"

"A Diesel locomotive," he said. "A brand new one. That was its horn."

"It doesn't sound right for a train," I said.

He just looked at me.

"Mama always says trains mourn for the crossroads," I said. "That one didn't mourn. It squawked!" I felt cheated somehow. More than that, I felt unsettled.

"Diesels sound different," my grandfather said. "They use a big air horn, not a steam whistle. Gonna be a lot of Diesels, from now on." He was checking to make sure Earl's rifle was unloaded. "Load your rifle," he said to me, the train already forgotten. "It's you turn to shoot."

I reached into my pocket for some .22 shells. But I knew the world was never going to be the same again.

4

Yellow Convertible Afternoon

I was four years old the year America started building new convertibles again, instead of tanks and bombers. But I don't know (and never knew) if the yellow convertible lodged deep in memory was one of those, or an older version kept patiently through the war years until new tires and gasoline were readily available again. Its shape – a long sleek nose and down-curved trunk – suggest the latter. I had a red toy convertible just like it.

Four years old is pretty young to begin to learn the secrets of surveillance. But the glossy yellow convertible, gleaming in the Southern summer sun, was easy to tail.

We tailed the yellow convertible in a taxi, my grandmother, my mother and me.

Lost in time is whether my mother was pregnant with my younger brother that year, or if he came along that day as an anonymous bundle in a baby blanket. How my grandmother funded a whole day's taxi ride I never knew.

We took the old wicker picnic basket stuffed with good food, and a brown-metal gallon jug of iced tea, the ice making a shushing sound every time the jug moved. There was no such thing as a fast-food outlet on every crossroad in those days; the first Dairy Queen (ice cream only) had yet to make an appearance in our hometown.

The yellow convertible led us out of Georgia into South Carolina across the Fifteenth Street Bridge above the Savannah River. We had staked out the woman's house, though of course I didn't know that term then: waited in the taxi, sweltering in the midday humid heat. I have often wondered what the cabbie thought about it all. I remember that he laughed a lot at tales my grandmother told, and seemed to enjoy the chase.

Sometimes we were close enough to see the woman's shining hair blowing free in the wind from the convertible's passenger seat. The driver's head was just an anonymous lump – but my grandmother knew who it was, by his car.

Sometimes the convertible was just a yellow dot topping one of the rolling hills of the South Carolina piedmont up ahead, when the cabbie fell back to give them space. I was the one who never lost sight of it – the cabbie commented that I must have the eyes of a hawk. I was secure in my far-sightedness and didn't understand why the grownups couldn't see what I could see.

To me it was all a grand adventure and a great mystery. I was very proud that they relied upon my sight to keep the yellow convertible under observation.

Swimming pools and roadhouses were the destinations chosen by the couple in the convertible – summer recreation and rendezvous points for Georgians trapped in the small hot city by the river. I had no idea what mysterious things went on in those places, but thought it must be something very grownup and fascinating.

We would find a wide-spreading oak or maple tree for shade, with a long view of the chosen location, and wait them out. My grandmother had the German binoculars her son had taken off a dead soldier, probably one that he had killed. It gave her a headache to use them when the taxi was moving, but at rest she braced them on the window sill and watched until her eyes watered, then surrendered them to my mother, with a running commentary of questions such as what do you see now, do you see them, what are they doing now?

I remember that my mother saw them swimming at one of the pools.

My grandmother saw them come out of a roadhouse holding hands and reported it grimly. He helped her into the car – Southerners did those things then – but my grandmother made it sound suspicious.

"Ruined her hairdo in that convertible, and swimming, but he don't seem to mind," she said sarcastically.

We spread our picnic lunch on a quilt beneath the cool shade of spreading oaks when it looked like the convertible's occupants were settled by a pool to bake in the sun for a while. My grandmother even had a plate and a glass for the cabbie. Cold fried chicken, her wonderful potato salad, egg salad sandwiches on white Colonial bread, iced tea from the jug, the ice cubes rounded now as they gradually melted, but the tea still achingly cold. The cabbie said it was the best iced tea he ever had.

With my farsightedness, I could see heat waves rise off the yellow convertible as it broiled in the sun outside the swimming club.

One thing that strikes me now is that the cabbie never asked my grandmother, the clear ringleader, what it was all about. Maybe she told him outside my hearing.

My uncle, the GI who returned with war trophies and medals, was head over heels about the woman with shining hair. My grandmother, protective of him as if he were still a teenager with a crush, wanted proof that the woman was still keeping company with her wartime paramour, who was one of those despicable 4-Fs. Four F sounded pretty bad the way she said it, with a sneer, though I had no idea what it meant. Keeping company was something grown men and women did when there was something grownup between them – that's all I knew about that.

What man in love ever truly understands how he is deceived? My uncle didn't believe his mother, and they argued about it.

My grandmother was a teenager when she lost her first true love to the Germans in the First World War. Mustard gas, she said, something so awful that only the awful Germans would use it on human beings. But I liked the bright yellow French's mustard she put on picnic sandwiches when it was so hot that Duke's mayonnaise might spoil. I was confused for a long time about how something that tasted so good could be fatal in the hands of the Germans.

My grandmother always said a girl got kind of crazy when her boyfriend was at the front – though she was forever silent about any craziness of her own in that first war. But the second big war was over now, her sons home alive if not unscathed, and craziness among her sons' girlfriends was no longer permitted. She had an iron code, my grandmother.

"He'll have to believe me now," she said with satisfaction, during the long surveillance.

Somehow in my callow mind, two-timing girlfriends melded into the hated Germans, neither worthy of my uncles' blood or tears. My grandmother conceded that the Germans were forever beyond her reach – but she could track down cheaters. She enlisted their sister, my mother, as a corroborating witness – of course most of these words and concepts were unknown to me at age four – but where my mother went, I had to go. So the bright yellow convertible came to live in my memory forever.

Yellow convertibles were rare, not all that hard to track, but that's grownup thinking about a boy's strange road trip. It was years before I knew such goings-on were a little out of the ordinary.

The ordinary end of the story was that the girl with shining hair became my aunt.

They stayed married his whole life.

She taught me how to draw. I loved trains then – what small boy didn't? – so the first things she showed me how to draw were locomotives. I got so good at drawing, thanks to her, that I won the first-place blue ribbon in a city-wide art contest by the time I was in the fourth grade. She sounded out words for me in the paperback Westerns my uncle read by the dozens and then gave to me. She was a good aunt.

I never knew what my uncle said to my grandmother about what we saw that day in the yellow convertible. But all their long marriage, my grandmother never forgave the violation of her iron code.

I never told my aunt about the yellow convertible afternoon.

5

Murphy Bed

The first Murphy bed I ever slept in was a mystery and a wonder, and it scared me. It folded down out of a closet in the wall, in an apartment on Yale Street in the city of St. Petersburg, Florida. The idea was to conserve space, I guess. I would awaken in the night sometimes and lie there waiting for the damn thing to snap up into the wall, imprisoning me upside down.

That was before television, but maybe I had seen that in a movie somewhere. Or maybe it was race memory: maybe humans aren't meant to sleep in beds that fold up into the wall.

I was in the fifth grade that year. I slept on one side of the Murphy bed, and my grandmother slept on the other. She snored. I don't remember where my mother and brother slept. We were in St. Petersburg on a house-hunting expedition for when my grandfather retired from the fire department up in Georgia. Things that happened in St. Petersburg are etched in my memory.

I broke my collarbone in a collision at first base during a pickup game before school, and couldn't try out for Little League or play baseball at all for the rest of the summer. Given my obsessive love of the game, it was a childhood tragedy of the first order.

I had to wear some kind of harness that held my shoulders just so, to avoid a cast. Even the open harness was almost insufferable in the humid Gulf Coast summer.

When we weren't looking at houses with a real estate agent, we took in the tourist attractions. I saw a hardhat deep-sea diver harvest sponges at Tarpon Springs, and kept waiting for his air hose to sever and kill him. I had seen that in a movie.

I smelled my first smoked fish in Passa Grille, and ate until I was stuffed, and even now my taste buds ache with the memory.

We didn't have a car – neither my mother nor grandmother knew how to drive – so we walked interminable miles cross-town to the grocery store, instead of taking the bus downtown and then back out. Buses didn't seem to run cross-town. I could only carry one sack because of my collarbone, and my shoulders both ached horribly on the long hurried marches home with perishable items in the heat.

One day a quart of orange juice, slippery with condensation out of the sack, fell to the kitchen floor and shattered, a crushing loss after the long walk. For decades my memory blamed me for the disaster, until my brother told me that he was actually the one who dropped the bottle and I should let go the guilt. It was a nice thing for him to say, even if he was just trying to ease the mind of his weird sibling. He never had understood how trapped up I got in past missteps.

Back then, I asked why the city could not install moving sidewalks, so we could just take a chair from the apartment and sit down, and whisk off to the grocery store. My grandmother and my mother laughed uproariously at that, and thought I had the most vivid imagination. Ever after, all they had to say to each other was "moving sidewalk" to burst into laughter.

The Murphy bed was a constant looming presence in my life. I was awake a lot in that Murphy bed after I broke my collarbone because there was no comfortable way to sleep in that damned harness. Sometimes when I shifted, I could feel the ends of the severed bone grind together.

Another vagrant memory: I almost stepped on a scorpion in the apartment doorway, coming back from the grocery store, and my grandmother killed it with her shoe, violent whacks.

Still another: I found two of my mother's paperback books tucked away in a drawer. They must have been early romance novels, except the characters engaged in more sex than you'd think such a book would have contained in the early 1950s.

Something hot and wild stirred in my blood when I read of the sex and the emotion, men and women making love, losing each other, finding each other again. Something that would live in my blood as long as my heart pumped it. My pulse raced in my ears when I read those books. I read them over and over, every chance I got, and looked forward to getting old enough to try what I read about it with both anticipation and terror: I was afraid of girls.

The second Murphy bed I slept in was in an apartment in Seattle, Washington, after I had lost a good deal of my fear of girls.

This second Murphy bed was a mystery and a wonder of a different sort entirely. It belonged to the girl I met the week before I was due to get out of the Army. I spent an awful lot of time in that second Murphy bed the only weekend that I was ever AWOL from the Army. Since I was so close to my discharge, nobody even noticed when I missed the morning roll calls.

Things that happened in Seattle are etched in my memory.

The bed labored and groaned under our lovemaking, that first weekend and later. We were young and tireless. Sometimes we even forgot to go out to get something to eat. After I was discharged from the Army, I rode the Greyhound forty miles to Seattle. I remember it as the slowest bus ride of my entire life, though I once rode a Greyhound from Georgia to Denver – and back.

I sat in the Seattle Greyhound coffee shop and waited for the girl with the Murphy Bed to get off work and come meet me to take me back to her place. I remember the slant of April light through the dusty windows, and the indescribable emotion I felt when I saw her come through the door.

"You are sooo fine," she would say in the afterglow of our lovemaking, drawing the word out in an indefinable way that sounded very exotic to my Southern ears. Her sparkling eyes in the shaded lamp glow were the center of a marvelous universe.

I loved taking down her office hairdo, scattering bobby pins everywhere, and the way her tumbled auburn hair would fan out on the damp bedding. Alabaster had only been a word in dictionaries until I saw her nude body by lamp glow in that Murphy bed.

It's a wonder that second Murphy bed didn't recoil and bounce us up into the wall, just like my childhood fears. Its springs complained loudly enough. And so did some of the other apartment dwellers, shouting through the thin walls. They probably wished the bed would pin us for a while, so they could have some peace and quiet.

Before my last night in that second Murphy bed, packing to go home to Florida, where the family finally moved after the St. Petersburg summer, I was nervous and almost irritable, because I was leaving. It was like one of my mother's long ago books – I was about to lose this girl, and had no confidence that I would ever find her again. I didn't want to leave. But I didn't know how to take control of my life and just decide to stay.

She sat quiet as a mouse in the corner, watching me with wide dark eyes. She hadn't seen this jittery, irritable side of me before. But she seemed to understand it. Later, in bed while she slept, I looked over and saw my packed bags from two years in the Army cluttering up the room.

I wished I could understand about choices. I still do.

That was the last night I ever slept in a Murphy bed.

6

1957 Palm Sunday on Palm Place

"The blue sky with large chunks of grey and white cloud, not actually threatening a storm but suggesting it. The cool sea breeze that seems to slake a thirst deep within your being..."

All these years later, the typed words are clear on the yellowed fragment of school notebook paper. The blue ruled lines have faded, but every keystroke still is clean and sharp.

Smith-Corona meant something then in typewriters, like Winchester in rifles and Singer in sewing machines. American brand-names stood for something in those days.

Kodak was another of those American icons. The emulsion on the Kodak snapshot is browned with time, but the image is sharp and clear, showing a fresh-faced boy sitting proudly behind the ancient Smith-Corona. I was wearing my Sunday sport coat with the Palm Sunday cross, fashioned out of real palm frond, pinned to the lapel.

The black office model Smith-Corona was ancient, even then. Its carriage return was on the right, a design that had been abandoned even then. For the information of those raised in the information age, the carriage return was the metal lever you used to push the carriage back to the left side of the page that you were typing, and to advance the sheet of paper around the roller to the next line, all in one. You could set the lever to single-, or double-, or sometimes even triple-space the lines.

"The bright rays of the sun, coming on an almost horizontal slant from the west, reflecting off the white buildings. The chirps of the birds in the oleander trees. The soughing of the breeze in the palms. The occasional high pitched cries of the gulls as they drift effortlessly, following the coast line..."

The typewriter was a gift from Mrs. Wimer, who lived across Palm Place in a garage apartment similar to ours. She worked in Jacksonville and drove a 1950 Mercury back and forth to the city from our little fire lane that was less than a block from the ocean. She was the first person I ever knew who had an old car repainted. The Mercury was a ghastly green now. But she liked it. She lived with her shut-in mother, who could not come down the stairs anymore. My grandfather would go over and visit with her mother about once a day, and I could hear her cackle as he told her stories from his sailoring and firefighting days.

I was fourteen when my grandmother told Mrs. Wimer that I wanted to be a writer, and Mrs. Wimer dug out the ancient Smith Corona. She gave it to me on Palm Sunday. I was immediately burdened with the seriousness of my obligation. Now I had to write something.

I looked around me at the upstairs screen porch where my brother and I slept, where we had taken down black curtains from the seaward windows when we moved here in 1954. The curtains were just like the ones my teachers pulled shut to black out a classroom when we were going to see a film. But these had been used to seal off any light from detection by U-boat skippers who lurked offshore to line up Allied shipping in their periscopes against the shore glow. The Germans had called the Atlantic coast of Florida "the shooting gallery" until full blackout was enforced. But none of that registered on me as worth the words then.

"The suddenness with which the tremendous pelicans loom from behind the houses on ocean front to glide by like silent planes. The crowded masses of arctic terns that fly in no particular order, their shrill cries mingling with those of the gulls. The bullet flight of the industrious little sandpipers, their wings a blur..."

I stopped hunting and pecking the keys and sat back, satisfied. My grandmother used her worn Kodak to record the event for posterity that Palm Sunday morning, and then we went to church. I was a writer.

7

Irish Eyes in Portland: 1966

She didn't believe I was a writer.

In those long-gone days it seemed that being a writer was something sexy, and men said they were writers as a way to score with women. I met her in The Embers, in Portland, Oregon. I was on a three-day pass from the Army. I was still very young toward women. The liquid courage of bourbon propped me up, and I asked almost all the unattached girls to dance. I asked her friend first. When we came back to her table, she challenged me about why I didn't ask her to dance first. Sober, I would have panicked, but the bourbon answered for me with a courtly bow, and an offer to mend the oversight immediately. When I led her to the floor, she fitted into my arms best of all the women I danced with that night.

I called her Irish right away.

It might have been the eyes, luminous and lovely in the subdued nightclub lighting. It might have been a vagrant memory that Mike Hammer had called a girl Irish in one of those hard-boiled Mickey Spillane detective stories I was reading then. For whatever reason, she liked the name. And she liked me. I moved to her table. After that, I danced with only her.

She didn't believe I was a writer. I was stung. I wasn't about to tell her I was in the middle of my two-year draftee hitch in the Army. It was not cool to be a GI in the flower-child and Vietnam era.

Come back to my hotel room if you don't believe me, I said, and I will show you my typewriter and my manuscripts. She had a merry laugh that made her eyes sparkle even more. Nice try, she told me. I was stung again. I was very young toward women. I hadn't meant that at all. Well, maybe I had.

When the lights came up at closing time, she left with her friends, but with a promise to call me the next day. They lived across the Columbia River in Washington State. The other side of the moon, if you didn't have a car. I wandered back to my hotel, disconsolate and alone. I wasn't particularly surprised at this; it was the way I usually returned from such forays. I knew she wasn't going to call me.

But she did. She called me from the hotel lobby. She had taken a bus across the river to see me, because her friend with the car had to work. She came straight up to my room, marching purposefully, to call my bluff. In those days a guest in a good hotel could always get the use of a typewriter. I had a big office model to work on, with half a novel scattered all around. I had been pounding away on Chapter 27 when she called. My editor at Doubleday had been urging me not to let the momentum from sale of my first novel die, just because I was stuck in the military.

She handled the typewritten pages almost reverently.

She sat in front of the big Royal typewriter and played with the carriage return, reading the interrupted last line I had typed. So you really are a writer, she said. I leaned toward her. She stood up into my arms. It was a long, tender kiss. My blood was drumming when she broke for air. Her color was high and her eyes sleepy. By god, I was going to get laid, if I could just figure out what to do next. But I didn't know what to do next. I hesitated too long.

Long enough for her to say those awful words: "You're so sweet."

How could I fondle her breasts then? I didn't think it would be sweet. I was extremely young toward women.

She eased out of my embrace and examined my battered old B-4 bag, bedecked with torn and stained travel tags, European and U.S.

"My, you do travel a lot, don't you?" she said wistfully. "I've always wanted to travel."

My head was spinning slightly. I had a mild hangover. She smiled at me and said something like poor you, and came back into my arms. We cuddled for a while. Then kissed some more, long, gentle kisses that began to heat up. I could feel the snare drums in my blood begin their tattoo again. My hands slipped down her back...

She leaned back, and put her fingers to my lips. "No. There will be other girls, in other towns."

Not with my luck, I wanted to grumble. But she took my silence for assent.

"We can't do this," she said. "You're not looking for permanence. For a" – she hesitated – "wife. Are you?"

That cooled my blood right down. A few sweet kisses and we were talking wedding bells? Hell, I thought this was the era of the Pill and free love. Couldn't we wait to select the bridesmaids until after I got laid?

But of course I couldn't just out and say that, or anything like that. It would hardly qualify as sweet, would it? So we talked. Or she talked. And I listened. The afternoon wore on. I learned about her Dutch ex-husband, and her Greek lover, and the several men since then. One of them she had seen walking on the sidewalk in front of this very hotel, when she had a car that was running, and she just pulled over and picked him up. She spent the weekend in bed with him. The kind of stories you tell somebody you happen to sit next to on an airplane, and know you will never see again. My unworthy, unsweet thought was, well what the hell's wrong with one more, then?

She fixed me with those lovely eyes. "There's something I must tell you."

Uh oh.

"I'm cold," she said.

I blinked and looked around. She half-laughed. "Not like that, silly. Your arms are warm." she sobered. "I mean I don't like sex."

What the hell was there to say to that?

She said after her last "experience," when she still had failed to achieve the elusive orgasm, she decided to just give sex up. Just like that; like she was talking about going on a diet. I was far too young toward women to suggest I might be able to help her accomplish what this coterie of others had not. And forever too young to not give a damn.

I suddenly felt the need for fresh air, and she agreed. We walked the rain-swept downtown streets arm in arm, heads together, and anyone would have thought us lovers. So much for appearances. She loved to pause and gaze at the travel-agency posters in the windows. She yearned to travel abroad, and intended to. We went into a cafe to have coffee, and sat for a long time, smiling at each other over all the shared intimacies. It felt comfortable, and edgy, all in one.

She liked the fact I smoked a pipe. "You should buy a pipe to commemorate our day." She talked like that; maybe she wanted to be a writer too, though she never mentioned it. "Or to commemorate Portland," she added. "You could have a pipe for every city. Every girl..." Her voice caught slightly, and then she forged ahead. "Every time you smoked your pipe, you'd think about that city."

Before too long she had to go; she worked a swing shift somewhere. Partings are never easy. The bus was already waiting when we got to the corner. Her lovely calves flashed beneath her dark raincoat as she ran to catch it. She turned at the door and called something out to me, but it was lost in the swish of passing tires.

Then she was gone.

A road not taken. But I still have my Portland pipe, Irish.

8

Interlude Lounge

It was a quiet little bar, dim, and the drinks were good. It seemed to draw much of its trade from the hotel patrons who walked in from the connecting door amid a brief blaze of lights from the lobby chandelier.

A woman, nicely dressed, sat on a bar stool, sipping her tall drink. Her back was erect as a drill sergeant. Most men who came through the door gave her the quick once over, saw her aloofness, and gave her a miss. Not this guy. Suave in his Navy blazer with a phony crest, grey slacks and loafers that almost glowed in the dark he slid right in beside her with a toothy smile.

Her head inclined approximately one millimeter.

He fiddled with the coaster the bartender put down on the way to get his drink. Then he picked it up and read the words.

"These are sayings from Poor Richard's Almanac." He had the studied, mellow tones of a radio broadcaster, and made it sound like a pronouncement.

"How nice," she said softly. "I hadn't noticed."

"Yep, sure are! Look, here's one: 'three can keep a secret if two of them are dead,' what do you think about that?"

"Interesting observation."

She tilted her glass and drank elegantly. Her every movement was elegant. More than one set of male eyes watched those movements, more or less covertly. He thought he was making headway. You could almost see his chest puff.

"Benjamin Franklin, you know," he said.

"Excuse me?"

"Benjamin Franklin," he confided. "One of our Founding Fathers. He was Poor Richard, did you know that?"

She tipped off the rest of her drink and stood in one smooth motion.

"Yes," she said. "I did know that."

The lobby door swallowed her before his lips could unsmile enough to cover his teeth. The bartender put his drink down on the coaster.

"Say," the man in the blazer said, "couldn't we get a little music in this place?"

9

Christmas in Nassau, 1969

Zed-N-S plays "Little Town of Bethlehem." Our little Christmas tree twinkles merrily in our one-room "bedsitter."

The Police Band was very impressive today. They were changing the guard and serenading the British Governor and the Bahamas Prime Minister surrounded by various VIPs and dark-uniformed police officials in Rawson Square. The sky was wintry and gray, a chill breeze was moving from the bay that lent authority to the myriad Christmas decorations. I shot a few pictures with the Topcon 35mm that I purchased from Colin yesterday.

Colin is a Nassau original, short, stocky, myopic and razor-witted; a British ex-pat camera shop proprietor who loves his pint and the companionship at the Red Goat. His hands on a camera are those of a virtuoso. His comments shine beams of clarity into every obfuscatory corner of the high cabal of photography.

"You focus with your left hand, shoot with your right," he instructed. "Hold your left hand under, cupping, instead of over. There are two reasons: your elbows are in close on both sides, and if for some reason the camera slips out of your right hand, it is falling into your left."

The band marched slow-time, wheeling. The drums and horns broke into an unknown number that added crystalline shivers to the coldness of the day. Militant, brittle, the left-rise, left-rise beat of the marching time set the blood astir.

The Governor and men in the dark almost black uniforms and British garrison caps were on their feet at once, then the Prime Minister and the other civilians and the women. One of the Bahamians in uniform threw a horizontal blade-edged American salute against his British cap, British crop properly aslant beneath his other arm. The song crashed cymbally to a close, followed by another, softer thing. The music paused, and all the VIP-seaters sat back down...

The P.M. in his dark suit and pink button-down shirt was surprisingly short between the tall rawboned British Governor and his tall lady, in a pink flop hat and English-cut suit with proper hem length, regardless of fad. The P.M. looked – a trifle uncertainly, it seemed to me – to the lank Britisher, like what comes next?

And the band struck up God Save The Queen.

Everyone on the stand seemed rigid for one instant, attention on the Governor. With an exceedingly elegant uplifting of arms that never quite raised his shoulders into a Gallic gesture – and that ended with him standing at full attention – he at once accepted blame for his faux pas in sitting too soon, got back in gear, and invited, almost compelled, the assemblage back to their collective feet.

There was a moment. Colonial ruler and new colonial

leader, shoulder to shoulder, surrounded by both retinues. Each as new to these strange islands as the other, in the long window of history. One's people came on the quarterdeck and the other's came in chains, until the Britannic Majesty militated against the slave ships and decreed that chains forged in Africa should be sundered here.

Law and order, a flag that still has a spot on it for a Union Jack, and some government buildings on Rawson Square; the Queen was paid her due. Then the honorary division commander stood to report his troops.

The governor bent and spoke quietly to the P.M. The P.M. moved out front and center on the podium to accept the honors from that loyal precision. His, now, to command. On his nod, the rest of the ceremony rolled forward.

Orders: open rank, march – the drum major setting the beat with a strictured step. The bandleader behind, rigid, chin at port arms passing in review, absolutely British, tightly constrained within the rhythm. The last song was played slow-march, like a dirge: "Auld Lang Syne."

Once down the street, around, the marchers blending and meshing, turning, wheeling, reforming before the P.M. on his wooden stand with the marble queen on her marble throne above his head and the marble leaping fish below him in Rawson Square. Then away, slow-march, with a muted, muted flourish of trumpets and drums.

The natives and the tourists, the expatriates and the mulattos and blacks, the sensitive and the insensitive, moved away slowly, awkwardly. The band's spell faded, rather than was broken...

I went to watch the band and practice my camera work for Junkanoo, the island's Christmas festival, for which Shirrel got me a street pass. We named our Christmas kitten Junkanoo.

Colleen and I went out to Cable Beach and captured it for Wanda. White with a black-and-ginger saddle and a black-and-ginger tail, with a tiny white tip, and a black-and-ginger kind of helmet.

She was wild as a tigress when I caught her, looking back over her shoulder as she and her littermates ran from Colleen. Then she was quiet in the shopping bag for the ride home. Then curious in the apartment, then afraid, then hungry, then curious, then afraid, and so on.

"She's so-o-o purty." Wanda was all grins.

Junky has already tried to climb in bed, deduced that the bathroom was where her litter was, and is already used to being handled and demands it by getting underfoot constantly...now sits on her haunches in front of the Christmas tree, doing light speed-bag jabs with a blue ornament. I feel the danger of becoming a cat person...

Things have been pleasing this weekend. Up at 4:30 a.m. to go out to Lake Killarney to shoot ducks. No ducks, but I talked with some Italian croupiers from Paradise Island who came to shoot too. They handled their guns with such good manners and such care. I wondered if their fathers had been boatmen and guides on those rich men's duck marshes in Italy that Hemingway wrote about in *Across the River and Into the Trees.*

The Italians wore their bell-bottomed hip-hugging gigolo pants tucked into prosaic gumboots, and stylish light wool pullovers to break the chill of a lake dawn. They admired my camouflage coverall. "What do you shoot – a 16?" Yes. "Aren't those loads too light? No high brass?" They do okay, when I have anything to shoot at. "Didn't you see that water hen go right over you?" I try to only shoot ducks. "Ohhh – he only shoots ducks!"

Now my Spanish double stands muzzles-down in Wanda's Norwegian gumboot, shiny slick with WD-40. Zed-N-S continues playing Christmas carols. The neighbor is taking a woman to bed, noisily, after being out all day at a Jack Nicklaus golf school. Wanda gives Junkanoo a Christmas ornament and she pursues it across the floor like a foosball player driving for a goal.

Christmas comes this Thursday, but we have it here Sunday night...

10

'Eyes Only' for Commander Bond

argo was playing chemin de fer. He had a fat pile of hundred-dollar plaques in front of him and half a dozen of the big yellow thousand-dollar biscuits. Domino Vitali sat behind him chain-smoking...by the way the people joked with him and applauded his coups he was obviously a favourite in the casino....

Remember Emilio Largo, Commander Bond? Remember that warm tropic night in the "Nassau Casino" that was really the Bahamian Club, when you met him across the baize and the chemin-shoe, with nuclear holocaust as the side-bet? Remember Domino, and the Cliquot rose and the fifty-dollar Beluga caviar with which you toasted her beauty and celebrated your forcing of Largo's hand at the table?

Well...

The rain comes down harder in the quietness of a tropic midwinter's day. Gray soft squally clouds eased in surreptitiously off the Gulf Steam in the night, and when the people of Nassau awoke, it was raining. The people of Nassau fear the cold rain, because getting wet can be a native's ticket to pneumonia and misery and maybe death. The rain slowed the tempo of the winter tourist season and muted the bright bird-of-paradise colours of the tourists, with black shiny bumbershoots that appeared out of nowhere and with cheap, hastily purchased plastic raincoats. The tourists appeared glum along Bay Street, which was penetrated from end to end by the musty barn odour of the wetted Straw Market.

And on West Bay, across from a stretch of public beach, sheltered just there by rain-slick coconut palms, overlooking the hushed greens of the harbour waters, the white stone red-roofed building takes it all impassively, bleached by island sun and stained repeatedly by past squalls. No one has whitewashed the stains for quite some time.

The architecture is vague Moorish, Commander Bond, a thing you might have noted and appreciated even in the midst of your set-to with SPECTRE. In point of fact, your biographer, the late Mr. Fleming, described it as *"a handsome private house...a well-run, elegant place that deserves its profit."*

Sad to relate, its handsomeness has been touched with the ravages of time that beset us all with the exception of some few folk-heroes like yourself, Commander.

Among the red tiles protecting the eaves, the rain finds empty gaps like a gum-line with teeth plucked by previous squalls, and drains unchecked down the stained watermarks of other rains. The arched canvas awning that protected guests from their cars up the graceful staircase to the front door is rotting now, and torn through where random palm fronds, knife-like on the force of a wind off the Atlantic, sliced through, or where an errant coconut, flung by those same boisterous winds like an assassin's grenade, punched a hole. Mildew crawls and spreads on the underside of the canvas with the untidy greed of maggots.

The solid glass front door at the top of the stairs stands still, undamaged, with the discreet initials of the club etched in the glass. But the casino is dead, Commander, as dead as your biographer. In this case an unpretty, ignominious death that you never could have foreseen when you trysted with Domino within its walls and purchased a packet of Players for her from the cigarette girl.

It should have caught fire in the midst of a run on the bank at the chemin-de-fer, or even, perhaps, that American travesty, the blackjack. Most romantic of all, perhaps the blaze should have interrupted a run against the Double-O numbers of the roulette that usually protected the house percentage so comfortably.

Symbolism that you would have appreciated, given your own Double-O designation, with which you attempted to protect the home islands – and the world – as securely as the roulette number protected the house percentage. So would your untold legions of fans that warmed their numbed twentieth-century sensibilities, during the long Cold War, with the bright flame of your individual swagger.

But the casino didn't die in fire. It just closed one day. The croupiers packed their grips and went back to Deauville or Monte Carlo or Las Vegas – or perhaps just across the harbour to Paradise Island. The pretty and the powerful stopped coming up the long, dwarf-cedar lined arc of the circular drive in Coupe de Ville taxis or in their Lotuses or Morgans or Alfas. They went elsewhere, and the stray potcake dogs and the mildew moved in.

The staircase carpet that softened the tread of the gamblers to and from their table fates is pulled away from its tacks now and rotting in the soft rain. Tyres swish by on Bay Street, but only rarely does some morbidly curious tourist wander through the drive to pause and wonder, and then accelerate away in his rented Triumph Herald or Fiat to brighter attractions down the road. The shrubbery stands like sentinels for some forgotten cause, surrendering its almost military botanical discipline reluctantly. It has grown shaggy with unbridled growth under sun and rain, amid the soft temptations of the surrounding ecology of sloth. The shadows of discipline amid the lack of manicuring somehow accentuate its faithfulness to the brighter days, when some green-thumbed drillmaster marshaled it to delight the eye of the rich and famous.

The graceful curve of the handrail that steadied inebriated guests to the tables – or giddy happy winners and traumatized losers away – peels long silver slivers of paint onto the sodden carpet. A muddy Canada Dry bottle and crumpled aluminum foil, residue of some workman's lunch perhaps, mock the rose and caviar of times past. Panes of glass and slats of jalousie are missing from the windows, blank spaces either boarded-up with cheap lumber at the beginning of the decay, or left open now, admitting the damp and the rot into the building's interior. Puddles and soggy Kleenex and a crumpled

Kentucky Fried Chicken box litter what was once a billiards-smooth lawn.

The natives love to hang out at "the Kentucky," Commander, as they call the fried-chicken emporium in town – just as the rich used to say "the club" about the casino – sitting on their Honda motorbikes at the curb since real estate is too precious to permit a parking lot there. Perhaps it is best you never return, Commander, to see what has become of the elegance you knew.

Largo turned round to face Bond...He said quietly, "But you are hunting me, my dear fellow. You are pursuing me...

Bond...said, "When I came to the table I saw a spectre...."

History tells us, Commander, that your late biographer worked in Intelligence in the last good war, against the Nazis. That he actually proposed, as an operation against a Nazi spy paymaster, the scheme you executed years later against Largo in Nassau. The stodgy Circus, it is related, turned him down. Never mind that your clerkish folk-hero counterpart, the incomparable Smiley, would have pursed his lips at your lack of tradecraft and polished his spectacles with his tie in disapproval.

Was it really the Special Executive for Counterespionage, Terrorism, Revenge and Extortion, in the form of the Commie paymaster Largo, to which you referred, hubristically alerting your prey as you banco'ed him three times in a row?

Or could it have been this rain-washed, blank-eyed spectre of a casino that sparkled and shone with lush life that dangerous night, a vision of the mortality that overtakes even well-run gaming houses and the chroniclers of heroes?

Never fear, Commander Bond. The pretty and the powerful have found other watering places around the world. Other chemin-shoes are slithering cards of victory or defeat across the baize. Cliquot and Beluga are far more expensive now, wherever it can be purchased. But the pretty and the powerful still buy it. It may be that somewhere the bill will go on a covert expense account even now. Intelligence budgets still are, for the most part, dark to prying auditors. Perchance some of those covert funds still are washed through the Royal Bank of Canada on Bay Street, as in your time. Such institutions, unlike well-run gaming houses, are nearly as immortal as you.

And Nassau will never forget you, Commander Bond.

11

Coffee Break at the Blue and White Café

"It was irritated," she said. "I'm going to tell him, too. But not until after Christmas. I don't want him to feel obligated, you know? He would feel obligated if I told him now. I'll wait until after New Year's to tell him. But I knew I wasn't going to get a diamond, and it irritated me to hear Joe telling me that I was. You know? I mean hearing from everybody in town that you're going to get a diamond when you're not going to. I'm the only one in town that doesn't know I'm engaged. If he even hands me a box that looks like a ring I'm just going to give it back to him without opening it."

"That's awful."

(Meaning awful about hearing it from somebody else, her friend meant, not about rejecting the box.)

"I wouldn't tell him about it before Christmas, you know. That'd be a dirty trick." Giggle. "You know? Awful. It would be a rotten trick, really rotten, because then I *know* he would feel obligated. I was irritated, though. I mean, just why bring the whole subject up at all? I would just as soon it would stay completely closed. You know?

Joe called me up at school to ask about it, he said I heard you and Don are engaged, and I said that's more than I know. You know more about it than I know, and he just laughed."

"That's terrible!"

"I wouldn't bring it up now, though, because I don't want him to feel obligated, and he would probably feel obligated and go right out and do it, and I *know* he doesn't have the money. I *know* that. I just wish the whole subject hadn't come up, that's all, and it would be a dirty trick." Giggle. "I'll wait to do it though because it would be a dirty trick. I don't want him feeling obligated."

"He'd do it too."

"*I* know! *I* know he would. He would feel obligated, wouldn't he?"

"He'd be obligated all right. He'd do it all right."

"I don't want him to feel obligated. He would, though, wouldn't he?"

"You know he would."

"It would be a dirty trick." (Giggle.)

"A really dirty trick, because you know he would feel like he had to. He told me he was, and..."

"Did he tell you not to tell?"

"Well...no. But you know he didn't want me to tell."

"He probably knows you would. He probably told me just because he knew you'd tell me that it wasn't going to be a diamond, so I would know. But he knew I wouldn't tell him I knew. *I* won't tell him. But he gets it back anyway. *I'm* not going to open it."

"It would be a dirty trick to tell him before Christmas Eve, because you know he'd go and change it."

"I know he would. And he can't afford it. He just doesn't have the money. I ought to, but I'm not. It would be a really dirty trick and I really am irritated, but I really shouldn't tell him until after New Year's."

Giggle. "Oh wouldn't it be dirty though?"

Giggle. "It would be a dirty trick all right. I was irritated. I was *so* irritated. You know?

Giggle. "It really would be dirty, all right."

Giggle. "It would be really dirty. A dirty trick."

"Well, we better go back. We've got to get those letters out. You're not really going to do it, are you?"

Giggle. "It *would* be a dirty trick, wouldn't it?"

"It would be awful to pull that at Christmas. You know he'd be obligated to do it."

"I don't want him to feel *obligated.*" Giggle.

Giggle. "He would, too."

Giggle. "I'll pay for the check."

12

Brave New Security

(being a story that died on the editor's spike)

They are citizens of another time and place, very ordinary citizens for the most part, of what history is beginning to assert was an extraordinary time and place. When they confront the time and place in which the rest of us live, as exemplified by the smoked-glass-and-steel tower of the Harrisburg Federal Building in this year of 1971, they just don't understand what they find.

What they find is security.

Not Social Security – that's what some of them are coming to this building to see about – or Medicare, or veteran's benefits, because those kinds of offices are in the building.

They encounter what the military calls "physical security."

That means armed, uniformed guards and doors locked where they have never been locked before during business hours; and sign-in registers; and having to tell the guards your business. Each federal structure in the land has become an armed citadel, like a beleaguered embassy in some faraway place with a strange-sounding name and hostile natives.

Federal building managers, whose worries used to be tornadoes and leaks in the roof and keeping the central air and heat working properly, have put on another hat – "my cop hat," the federal building manager here calls it, with a twist to his lips. They schedule their new armed forces for small-arms training and sessions in arrest takedown procedures, and anticipate the arrival of a special flying squad of heavily armed shock troops that will be on call very soon. The phone number of the bomb disposal squads is at the top of their personal address books.

But older citizens, who were being born about the time Wilbur and Orville Wright were trying to fly box kites with motors down in Kitty Hawk – and who, at about age seventeen, went to Europe to fight a war to end all wars, or waved goodbye to the ones who went – can't seem to grasp this thoroughly modern world.

They climb the low steps to the wide entrance – four big glass doors wide – and fumble at the heaviness of the doors, realizing only belatedly that they are all locked. Sometimes they try to peer through the artfully darkened glass. Sometimes they keep trying until they find the one that the security guards have decided to leave unlocked for that day – on a rotation known only to them.

Sometimes they simply turn and trudge away, evidently deciding that their government is closed for the day.

"You see that a lot," says a guard wearing the unfamiliar new General Services Administration uniform. He mans the check-in booth that has become a permanent encampment in the wide-open lobby, whose architect never penciled in checkpoints. He sits right by the register you must sign now to enter the building.

"They just never learn," he says, peering through the wide glass windows at the bright day outside, invisible to anyone approaching the building. He says he thinks it peculiar that they won't keep trying until the find the open door.

He frowns at a ventured observation that they are just confused because a government of the people, for the people, and by the people, that built a building with four wide doors so a lot of those people could get in to see it, has suddenly decided to lock three of them, to try to make sure that some people don't.

Most of the elderly finally catch on, like others, to the musical doors setup. It's called "movement control" by the security-conscious. Once inside they are invariably flagged down by a man wearing an unfamiliar blue uniform with a brown Sam Browne belt. Invariably, because they walk right past him as if he is invisible and head for the elevators, as if they owned the place. Once – not that long ago, really – citizens felt that way about federal property, constructed with taxpayer dollars.

"Got some identification?" the guard challenges brusquely, irritated by being ignored by every oldster who comes in.

Brusque or sometimes polite, the challenge draws the identical blank stare from each oldster submitted to it for the first time. Almost as if the wall had spoken, or the carpet. Ever since these rare citizens can remember, they have gone unchallenged about their daily affairs with a personal freedom the pharaohs might have envied, but the

Roman Senate would have approved. More than half a century of it, longer than some totalitarian dynasties survive, freedom to go about their private business as an ordinary daily experience.

Ended now. Movement *control,* now.

They just don't know what to make of it.

The little old lady was incredibly tiny, bundled in heavy winter clothes to her ankles, hair like spun silver. She just looked at the towering muscular guard, not comprehending. It may have been the first time in the fullness of her years that someone had doubted that she was herself.

"Your Medicare card, show him your Medicare card," said the old lady's companion – a woman with plenty of iron stippling her own dark hair.

"Oh."

The little old lady, still wondering what it was all about, began to fumble in her purse.

"Now, what about you?" the guard said to the younger woman – old enough to be his mother.

"Oh, I'm not going to see the Medicare. I'm just along for the ride." She took the old woman's arm and started off.

"You don't get in, you don't show some identification," the guard said, stepping in front of them.

"But I'm just along for the ride!"

No matter. Rules are rules, orders are orders, and the guard is just following his. She could have a purse full of plastique or a Bren gun under her bulky overcoat, after all. She shows him her Harrisburg Library Card and he makes a judgment call: good enough.

Searching by the guards is so far reserved for packages and briefcases. On some special occasions, for women's purses, which is another whole culture clash by itself. But on a day when the Nixon Administration's courtroom war against the antiwar left is on hold, the metal detectors are not turned on and there are no body searches. Just the drab routine of challenge and identification.

"Where you going, lady?"

The blank stare again. Another four-foot-tall little old lady, who looks like everybody's great-grandmother.

"The social security," she responds slowly. Then, the words tumbling over herself as if she fears that she has committed herself irrevocably, "No, no, the revenue. The revenue."

"Internal Revenue Service?"

"The revenue." She nods impatiently, now that she's got it right. "The revenue. Listen, I got my return and it didn't..."

"Lady, I'm not the Internal Revenue."

"You're not?" She regards him with obvious distrust. "Where are they then?"

He gives her a floor and room number.

"You go up the elevator," he says.

"I don't like elevators. Where are the stairs?"

"You can't go up the stairs."

"It's okay. I'll just go up the stairs."

"You can't go up the stairs, the doors are all locked. Regulations. You got some identification?"

"I'd rather go up the stairs. I don't trust those elevators."

"They're all right. Could I see some identification,

please?"

"Stairs are still better," she says, and starts for the elevators.

"Anything you have," the guard says. "A social security card, driver's license, anything."

"Young man, I don't have a driver's license. I don't drive. Never have. I don't trust automobiles. Why should you want to see my driver's license if I don't have one?"

"Anything you have," the guard says doggedly.

She is still walking toward the elevators. As the guard follows her, another older woman comes briskly in off the street and heads for the first-floor cafeteria, just off the lobby.

"Whoa, whoa!" the guard calls. "Where do you think you're going?"

"To get a cup of coffee," she says, as if that is the most obvious thing in the world.

"Well, you can't."

"I can't? Why?"

"Rules. You can't just come in off the street and go in there. You gotta have business in the building. You got business in the building?"

"I want a cup of coffee."

"Go somewhere else. You can't get it here."

He turns his back on her outrage and catches up with the little old lady headed for the revenue at the elevators.

"Social security card, anything," he says.

Finally she comes up with her Internal Revenue Form for 1971. "You see, it doesn't make sense..." She holds it toward him.

He scans the form for her name, nods officially, and

goes back toward the door, where younger, more socialized citizens have dutifully lined up to sign in and show their drivers' license or whatever. Then he remembers and turns back.

"You gotta sign in, Lady."

"What?"

"You gotta sign your name."

"I thought you weren't with the revenue."

"Lady, just come back here and sign your name and it'll be okay," he says. She follows him back to the entrance. "Just sign in right there. Here's a pen."

She signs, head down, finally cowed. "Is that all I have to do?"

"That's it, that's all. You can go on up there now and get it all straightened out."

She heads back for the elevators and a bystander asks her what she thinks of all the new security precautions.

"The what?" she asks. Then, "Do you trust elevators?"

"What do you think about – you know, all this signing in and all?"

She wags her head. "I just want to see the revenue and get it straightened out, that's all. I wish you didn't have to use the elevators."

13

Flea Bag Hotel

It was one of those stifling humid mid-summer days that you get in Central Pennsylvania in a city right on the Susquehanna River. Market Street was a heat-blasted tunnel, the few pedestrians who hadn't taken cover wilted and lethargic. It seemed like a long hike from the courthouse back to the newsroom. A jury had gone out, eaten their county-paid lunch, and come back and convicted a college student of desecrating the American flag for sitting on a plastic one at a demonstration while wearing a T-shirt describing America as the Fourth Reich.

I broke my trek at Duane the Bookseller's, one of my Market Street hangouts where more than one street rumor had led me to a good story. Duane told me that he had fallen heir to the fleabag hotel that rises four brick stories above his fire-marshal-bedeviled stacks of used books. (The sign on the door reads Smoking on These Premises is Forbidden by The Fire Marshal and Common Sense.)

The hotel is closed down, the last down-and-outers forced out, and Duane was having in antique dealers to find and bicker over surprising wash stands, library tables, desks, chairs, bedsteads scattered through the narrow rooms with paper window shades. He invited me for a tour of the dim and surprisingly cool premises.

One of the first mattresses I saw lay without a bedstead beside a wall scored and pitted with caked-on vomit so ancient it was odorless. The flow marks of the lava-hard eruptions – untouched by cleaning agent – indicated probable daily eruptions, increasingly flecked with rusty brown.

A carefully burrowed out hole in another mattress revealed a plastic hairbrush. Magazine cutouts of pretty meadows wallpapered one dismal hole above the street.

Coat hangers everywhere. Legions and legions and legions of coat hangers, enough to stock a good-size laundry. Did the damn things breed in the dark?

Check stubs and window-paned envelopes from Medicare, "the welfare," insurance companies, hospitals – then a lone receipt from a jewelry store showing ten dollars paid and a ninety-dollar balance, not identifying the purchase.

One filthy plastic syringe – and a letter from the dead letter office containing a flimsy plastic card case stuffed with cards saying "I am not drunk. I am diabetic."

There was one room they all by common consent, according to Duane, used as a urinal. Shoes made sucking, smacking sounds on the coated boards. On another floor was a pickle jar full of yellow fluid, stinking the room with an aggressive odor to cut the dismal mustiness of disuse.

A busted spinning rod, the reel long since vanished. A Playboy centerfold with full, hard-nippled breasts, thumbtacked beside a National Geographic centerfold of a caravel in full canvas running before a light gale. Then a long, old-fashioned hunting mural – hounds and hunt club, marsh keeper carrying a rabbit-ear black powder double with a retriever beside him.

"They tried to make their lives less drab," Duane remarked.

Next a bright beer advertisement cut out of a magazine, showing a harness race. Then a wide photo spread from the New York *Daily News,* sequential shots of Cassius Clay being hammered by Joe Frazier.

A room without artwork – but the bed stacked ponderously with about 500 Philadelphia *Inquirers* – mostly the Sunday edition – with still more stacked along the walls and piled on the battered furniture.

"He slept with 'em," Duane said.

In one room, an ironing board. Two rooms later, across the hall, the carton it came in, looking newer than the board.

The corridors were almost too narrow for my shoulders.

"One man," Duane reported, "retired and moved in here and never saw the light of day for five years, and died. He was in perfect health when he came."

Every door had at least two locks that were not original, some as many as four or five – many of them padlocks. An abandoned, silver, sturdy Yale sat open on a washstand.

Naked razor blades scattered here and there. Boxes of old clothes at the landings, waiting disposal. One shirt on a hanger, overlooked, a white Arrow, size 16-16 1/2, with rusty stains down its front.

"The police were always here. They were always fighting. Standing here with blood pouring out of their ears, mouth, nose, waiting for an ambulance. No blacks were allowed. Some floated through, but no tenants. There were three women who kind of circulated between all the men. Awful, ugly, fat, old – terrible hags. One of them was black, but the landlord said *that* was okay."

Original Gideon Bibles. One book called *The Philistine*. A 1965 *Outdoor Life*. A couple of car magazines. A pair of small stiff black leather gloves, all that remained in a sturdy wooden wardrobe the antique dealers were interested in. A hand-cranked machine for making filter cigarettes. Salt and peppershakers, and an ashtray or two, from restaurants all over town. In another wardrobe, a grey and black houndstooth check topcoat in almost-new condition.

Most of the furniture was cheap rickety crap, covered with the same thick dust as the few interesting pieces. Old-fashioned wooden TV consoles, gutted, stared blankly; used as cupboards, Duane said. On an inner door, a restaurant fork through the hasp of a padlock. Protected by the forked lock, an overdue medical bill from Geisinger Medical Center in Sudbury: "Did you forget...if you have mailed your remittance, please disregard this notice."

And on and on, until it all began to blur.

"Interesting how some people end up, huh?" Duane said when we were back in the bookstore.

I purchased two paperbacks for the weekend, The *Doomsters* by Ross McDonald and *Martin Eden* by Jack London. Only later did I wonder if my selections were affected by my tour.

14

Sunbathing Party

One of those dead days in the newsroom when the phones pause in their eternal clamor, nobody is pounding out a story against a deadline, and the mild spring weather outside beckons. All I needed was an excuse, so when Ron asked me for a ride I was ready to go.

He had a make-work assignment, a story about how slow intra-city mail delivery is in the face of new postal rate-hikes. He wrote a bunch of letters to himself and was going to post them all over town and then report how long it took them to come in. But they yanked his driver's license when he copped a plea to marijuana possession, so he needed a chauffeur.

We were over on the West Shore, finished with the mail boxes, when we noticed a road that looked interesting, roofed over with bright hot green leaves that reminded me of the Foret National near Fontainebleau, where I never took a girl with a blanket and a picnic basket and always wished I had.

The road dead-ended at a rippling creek, wide-watered, bright in the sun, the ruins of a bridge's pilings slumping in two eddies of their own making.

"We've interrupted a sunbathing party," Ron said.

We had parked the car by what looked like the topside of some mysterious underground installation surrounded by cyclone fence. Vents and apertures poked up out of the green. We walked down to look at the beach. Ron was ahead. He turned back, looking embarrassed. I thought immediately that he'd spotted a couple making the two-backed animal in the spring sun.

But it was a pair of bikini-clad women, sunbathing, lying sun-drugged on their towels beside an old Chevelle. They peered at us as if the ground had disgorged us.

"We didn't mean to intrude, honest," Ron called out. "We just came to look at the water."

No reply; they just continued to stare in that bemused fashion. One turned off her belly and sat up. I saw suntan oil gleam along her flat, browning belly. She was the blonde in yellow; her companion was a pale brunette in white. Now they were both sitting up, clasping their arms around their knees.

"Quite a show for anyone over there across the creek," I said.

Across the creek, past the spreading shade trees that lined the shore, I could see an International Travel All parked beside turned brown earth where a field began.

The girls watched us and we not-watched them. I felt acutely uncomfortable. They were taking turns watching us now, covertly and openly by turns. We left abruptly, without discussion, and they watched us all the way out of sight onto the path that led to the road.

I pointed out that I had felt no negative vibrations from the girls. They weren't anxious, they were curious.

"That brunette now," Ron said. "Wow!"

"Maybe we should have gone over and talked to them," I said.

"They weren't against it."

"They weren't high school. Too old," I said. "They didn't feel like college either."

"They might have been – no, they weren't nurses, either," Ron said.

I drove up the steep bank back to the road, the company Chev laboring on the incline.

"I bet they thought we were a couple of fags looking for a place," I said.

"We should have tried them," Ron said.

"They were expecting it at first. You know they thought we saw them from the road and came down."

"When I looked over, I saw that brunette looking right at me. She was still sitting up. I couldn't see the other one."

"They wouldn't be teachers," I said. "The kids are just getting out of school now. Office girls, playing hooky."

"Office girls. That's what I thought too," Ron said. "Maybe we should go back."

"Not now. At first maybe, but now they would be suspicious. It would make them nervous for us to go away and then come back like that."

Our casual outing after dealing with the letters had gone stale on us. Ron got randy and wanted to go back really badly. I remembered that I still had to get my vehicle out of the shop. Then he remembered that he was obligated to go see "The Cross and the Switchblade" because he now is tripping on Jesus, as he puts it, a reformed head since his brush with the law, and such viewings are required by his new friends.

"So it's all academic," he said. "But, speaking academically, I abhor the shit out of it."

"I'm glad of the opportunity," I said. "I'm just glad to be shown that life will twist on you when you least expect it. Just the opportunity has made my whole afternoon." "They were already made," Ron said. "Warm spring day, their first time in their bathing suits, first time out in the sun. All we had to do was be there."

"We were there," I said. "And we left."

"They were half-made already. I may go home and beat my wife."

15

A Rodeo in Harrisburg

The spring day was warm and clear and lovely, with that good old feeling of the road moving up to meet you, just relishing the feel of motion for motion's sake and enjoying the roadside greening of Pennsylvania's deciduous forests.

I took a short side trip into a Lancaster (Lankster they pronounce it back here) shopping mall to get a cleaning cloth for my sunglasses. I asked at the cash register for the quickest way back to the highway toward Harrisburg.

I went to Harrisburg once, the sales girl said. Somebody else drove. To tell you the truth, I didn't pay attention to how to get there. We were going to the rodeo.

She said Harrisburg like you might say Amarillo or Pendleton, or some other far away and fabled home of the rodeo. Wide-brimmed Stetsons, bulls raging out of the chutes trying to kill their riders, bucking broncos! Rodeo! In Harrisburg, Pennsylvania? But that's what she said.

16

Sunset Boulevard

Thursday afternoon, I rented a station wagon from Budget at LA International and they gave me a Union 76 map of the city when I asked them how to get to Western Avenue. On the map it all seemed very simple and it was. Century Boulevard out to the San Diego Freeway, then north to the Santa Monica Freeway, east on the Santa Monica, get off at the Western-Normandie exit, then turn left – north again – and keep going until you hit the 700 block; simple.

Hell, too simple – I pass up the 700 block and keep driving. Traffic is clogged and sluggish, moving by fits and starts. I am inclined to fight it and then wonder why. I'm not going far, just back to 713 Western Avenue, and I'm not in a hurry, I just need to check in before they knock off for the day.

So I relax and let the traffic carry me, let the unfamiliar rhythm of the traffic lights catch me and hold me while the impatient locals force their way on through. LA is the first place I've ever seen five or six cars turn left against a red light, nose to tail, like circus ponies, daring the oncoming traffic to try to break in.

Los Angeles, California: Raymond Chandler country, if

you're a detective novel fan like me. Hell, Jack Webb country, if you grew up with a black-and-white television set for brains, like me. This is the city, dum de dum dum – Los Angeles, California.

I don't work here. I'm not a cop.

I don't even know what I'm doing here, driving a big clunky County Squire station wagon north on Western Avenue, rented so I can stack the rear with union campaign brochures designed to convince Los Angeles city workers that they need a union.

I never set out in life to be a PR man, and if I had, unions would not have been my first choice for which to do PR. On top of that, if I made a list of all the cities in the world I didn't want to work in, LA would be right at the very top. Right there with New York City and Chicago and Washington, D.C.

So I interviewed for a union PR job in Washington, D.C., and they hired me – and sent me here. Life is what happens when you forget to pay attention. I may as well take a few minutes to look around my new neighborhood before I report in.

A traffic light catches me. A girl in greasy Kit Carson buckskins is standing on the street corner with her thumb out, hitchhiking down the cross street. She must not be doing too well at it. She's leaning against the signpost like she really doesn't have much hope. I look at the green street sign: Sunset.

"Well Kookie, Kookie, lend me your comb," I say through the windshield to the girl.

Her response is amazing. She comes to life, bounces off the curb, tries my right hand door. It isn't locked; I'm just off the plane in LA, still careless.

She leans in the door. I get a flash of big dark eyes before her abundant hair cascades around her face, shutting out the sunlight.

"Hi there," she says.

"I'm not going your way, kid," I say.

"That's all right," she says brightly, and slips into the car. "I'll go yours, Pops."

Pops. I'm thirty years old.

Horns blare. The light has changed. I let the Ford wagon drift around on Sunset, up to the curb.

"Thought you weren't headed this way," she says.

"I'm not. I'm just turning around. I've got an appointment back there. I was just cruising because this is my first time in LA."

"Appointment can't keep, huh?" She turns toward me so the Kit Carson fringes gape open to reveal a T-shirt full of unbridled breasts.

"For God's sake," I say. "At four o'clock in the afternoon? Right here on the corner in broad daylight?"

She tightens up. "Look, Pop – you some kind of weirdo, maybe? Some straight, gets his kicks off just talking?" She looks back at the intersection. "Damn!"

"What's the matter?"

"You've made me miss a whole signal change. You know how many cars go by that corner? I do. Probably a hundred thousand cars a day, that's how many. And you still get the nuts. That's what a billboard salesman told me."

"That you still get the nuts?"

"No, about the cars, stupid. How would a billboard

salesman know about guys like you?"

"How would anybody?" I say. "Look – you better get back to work now. You've probably missed at least five hundred and ten cars by now, and I'm blocking a driveway."

"You're really weird," she decides. "Where you from, anyway?"

"Florida."

"It figures," she says, and is gone in one nimble contortion, the door slamming smartly shut behind her.

I put the wagon in drive and move on down Sunset, looking for a street to swing back toward Western now that I have been officially welcomed to the city.

17

Los Angeles Pickup

The girl was wearing a tan mini suit. She asked the people at the bar if Weird John had been there tonight. The fattish, balding bartender thumbed his hairline 40's mustache and said that was a horrible name for a person.

"That's an awful name." He said it over and over. "Awful. Just awful. What an awful name."

"What you want him for?" asked a guy at the bar. "Yeah, he was here."

"He came by here to sell me a ring before, and the other bartender threw him out before I could pay him."

The bartender told somebody he was divorced – two years. I got no problems now. Call me Eddie. They went thataway. My problems. I pay my rent, have my fun, go to the races. One day I made $400 touting, you know?"

The girl in the tan suit ordered an orange juice, "because the doc has put me off liquor. I got an ulcer working. We live outside L.A. Where you from?" she asked the bartender. "Texas?"

"Texas? Hell, I'm from Joisey. Can't you tell? How long you been living out there?"

"Five years."

"Who's us?"

"My sister and I."

"I got a place in town. Eighty bucks a month."

"We're paying one-seventy for a two-story house."

"You oughta see my place then."

"Maybe I should."

"I even got orange juice in the fridge."

18

Papa Choux

The motel was on Olympic Boulevard, an ordinary enough place by LA standards, if you didn't count the birds. The whole damn inner courtyard was a gigantic wire-caged aviary, dripping in tropical foliage and full of bright-colored jungle birds enough to stock a Trader Horn remake. They were so damn noisy that you couldn't hear the traffic on Olympic, even during the LA rush hour. The atonal avian night chorus was just tuning up when I walked down the boulevard in search of dinner.

Papa Choux sat well back from the traffic on a large landscaped, slightly elevated lot, up a wide, curving drive that led under an elegant canopy. With the lighted palm trees and greenery, and the liveried valets, you half expected to see white-side-wall Packards and vintage roadsters driven by platinum blondes, like a Raymond Chandler novel. But this was 1973 and Mercedes and Jaguar seemed to be the LA flavors of the month.

The appetizer surprised me: liver cheese with crackers. The first taste threw me back in time to bright Florida days, the deep backwaters of the Intracoastal Waterway beneath the vast gray-green canopy of Spanish-moss-draped oaks. And Parkhill Chaires and I, balancing our fishing rods on our bikes down the shell-paved road to fish the dark water for largemouth bass.

For some reason I always had liver cheese sandwiches in a paper sack for lunch, and a brown Thermos bottle with a red stripe on it full of chocolate milk. My grandfather got the liver cheese at the farmer's market.

We caught no fish and got mosquito-bitten despite smoking the cheap Cuban cheroots to ward them off that Parkhill bought back in bundles from his Havana trips. Parkhill was a couple years older than me, having been held back in school not for lack of smarts but lack of interest, and had already been to Havana, first with his dad and then on his own. He inflamed my imagination with his smirking tales of his solo excursions to the fleshpots of that fabled city. Chocolate milk, Cuban tobacco and liver cheese sandwiches – no wonder that by the time I graduated high school I was taking medicine to tranquilize my stomach.

But Papa Choux' is a pedigreed sort of liver cheese. I order Jack Daniels Black Label to wash it down. My stomach is stronger these days.

"We only pour Jack Black," the waiter says. "It's the very best."

"Alone?" the German headwaiter asks me now.

"Yes," I say. "Unfortunately."

"Perhaps later," he says. "For the night is early."

"There's always hope."

"Particularly here in the City of Angels," he says pertly.

A strolling violin and accordion strike up "Wiener Blut," and Germany seems suddenly a lot closer to LA.

I order a bottle of Paul Masson Grenache rose to go with steak, baked potato and asparagus. The French wine steward – even older than the headwaiter, silver-haired, very dignified – says California wines improve each year.

"In one hundred years, they will be great wines. But we won't be around to enjoy them."

"I don't know," I say.

"So you'll stick around?" he says, laughing.

"Damn right."

The steak is tender. They don't even bother to bring a sharp knife. The full bottle works its magic. I take on a glow. It's not the Pommard I learned to love in Germany, but Pommard in California would destroy my expense account for a month. The players stroll. "Wunderbar." "Lili Marlene." Then American tunes that I tune out.

The iron-haired German headwaiter has such a presence he almost has to be an out-of-work or never-was actor. The French wine steward is almost oriental in gracious servitude. The sullen assistant waiter actually is Asian, Japanese by his look. The wine steward is surrounded by a two-third representation of the old evil Axis triumvirate, and Papa Choux is evidently Italian: the new United Nations of LA.

"Enjoy, sir," says the headwaiter, personally bringing me coffee. "Please enjoy."

The proprietor approaches, slicked back dark hair, suave in a dark double-breasted suit – Don Corleone in his salad days. How was everything?

"Beautiful," I say.

"I am Papa Choux," he says.

I stand to shake hands and give him my name, earning

a small neat bow for the courtesy.

"Thoroughly enjoyed," I say.

"Thank you very much."

Motif is red and back; wrought-iron lanterns on every table. The diners are well dressed, for the seventies – no leisure suits, no pants on the women. The German headwaiter waiter brings me a teak humidor of cigars.

"The owner's private stock," he tells me in a mock whisper. "Still Cuban. Don't ask." Not even Perkeo's in Heidelberg offered Cuban cigars.

"I grew up on Cuban leaf," I say. "I'm from Florida."

"Makes me very happy, sir."

City of the Angels for sure – and the night still is young.

19

Getting to Phoenix

I always liked that song "By the time I get to Phoenix" by Glenn Campbell, because the road trip he sang about seemed to originate in the city of angels and head east to Phoenix and Albuquerque and Oklahoma. It was the exact route—in reverse—that I had taken west before turning north for Washington State. The leave-takings and lost love at which Campbell's song hinted—well, perhaps the song spoke to me because I had my own version of that story all bound up in my California memories.

After a sojourn in the Pacific Northwest, I found myself, on October 30, 1976, on the way to Phoenix, coming down out of the rainy country. I would have a hard time imagining an unlikelier twist to my checkered career.

A lot of country had rolled under the tires of my orange VW Super Beetle that day. Some of the scenery was pretty dramatic, old abandoned cabins and mining claims, revealed by sagging scaffolding perched on hillsides. Then the junipers suddenly appeared and thickened and spread like an encamped army over the low rolling hills that once were the bottom of an inland sea. A rest stop information plaque spoke of the depths of that prehistoric sea, and the kinds of creatures that swam those lightless depths.

My imagination fired up. I saw some frontier youngster, quivering beneath the homemade quilts in a homesteader's cabin, squeezing his eyes tight shut to avoid seeing, through chinks in the cabin mortar, the eerie luminescence of deep-water, glowing-eyed things that swam by in the night when the ghost ocean reclaimed the prairie.

I could see his hardy and unimaginative father laughing at breakfast, in the safe morning sun, telling the boy that he only saw cattle moving by in the dark, their eyes reflecting dying embers from the fireplace.

The boy not contradicting his father, but mutely wondering how cows could swim above the roof peak, casting cold phosphorescent gleams down the cold chimney...

The sun left me south of Salt Lake City and I drove on into the dusk. South of one of those old-fashioned little highway towns that probably will become the next ghost town when the freeway down this way is complete, a big Ford Country Squire station wagon braked violently in front of me. I almost rode the tire-shrieking, whipsawing Bug up its tail pipe, but somehow got it stopped ten feet short of her tailgate.

The woman was okay. The mule deer doe she hit was not. One rear leg was a twisted mess with protruding bones and there was blood puddled under her while she lay stunned, breathing raggedly. Cars and trucks were blowing by at speed, even though I tried to slow them down with a waving flashlight. The doe reared up, and flopped, reared up, and flopped—all her legs were broken and jutting at awful angles. She was trying to flop out into the road in the direction she had been heading when hit.

I went and got the Model 88 out of its saddle scabbard in the VW. In the flickering headlights I tried to focus on her spine through the scope and achieved the distinction of missing at point blank range when I shot into the ground beside the thrashing neck. I placed a boot on the neck to hold it still and pressed the muzzle to the spine and delivered her from suffering.

I never dreamed my hand-loaded .308 rounds would wind up being used for euthanasia on a crippled mule deer in the far southwest corner of Utah.

Things got stranger. The run from Southern Utah seemed to detour through the Twilight Zone. North of the Grand Canyon, a whole herd of mule deer leaped into the road, all around and over the roof of the VW, hooves going by above the open sunroof, before I could even react. Then they ganged up on the far side of the road and stared at me where I sat at the end of my skid marks. I was wearing my tires out in panic stops.

Before too long I found myself navigating the vast Navajo reservation, dodging pickup trucks driven by highly intoxicated Indians on the way home for the night— or to another watering hole.

As a matter of fact, they *did* own the whole damn road. The only saving grace was that their shoulder-to-shoulder ramblings were taken in a leisurely manner. I could slip up behind one, time his gentle sweeps back and forth across the highway, and gun by on one side or the other, winding the little Bug up into the redline and away. Fortunately they were happy drunks and not annoyed; I got a couple of friendly waves as I downshifted by.

The final mind-bender came as I approached Flagstaff from the north—a set of headlights coming up fast and hard, making me thing either a belatedly angry Indian or a highway cop.

Neither: Bozo the Clown in full makeup, ruffled polka-dotted shirt and all, driving a big old Buick like a madman. He zoomed up beside me with that painted-on grin and white grease paint shining at me in the lights of his instrument panel, and under the paint I could see him chortling at my startled response. Weren't there horror movies that started like this?

He roared off into invisibility over the winding hills. Then a little while later as I plodded tiredly on, here he came again. Same pass, same chortle, same grotesque painted grin—and this time a saucy little salute—before he was gone again.

It is no exaggeration to say I contemplated pulling off and taking the .308 out of its scabbard behind the seat. Why the hell had he stopped out of sight and then strafed me again? Maybe Bozo just had to pee—or maybe he was screwing with me.

I never knew. Bright lights in the night advertised some kind of agricultural inspection station. As I was pulling into the lights, Bozo went prancing around his car—the only part of the costume missing was the clown shoes, and his feet in tennis shoes were big enough anyway—and hopped in and roared off. The inspector went through his routine with me about any vegetables to declare as if he was on automatic pilot.

"Did I imagine that a clown just came through here?"

"A lot of clowns come through here," he said in a slow

Western drawl, without any change of expression.

"But I meant—"

"Yeah, yeah—that one was actually wearing his uniform" he said, and turned and walked away.

I guess midnight duty on the Arizona border hardened a man.

By the time I got to Phoenix I was starving. When I sat at the counter of an all-night diner, I was surprised to see low ground fog blurring the lights off toward the city, like vapor rising off the wetlands of home. I said as much to the waitress and she just looked at me.

"That's dust," she said. "It never settles this time of year."

It looked like I had definitely gotten to Phoenix.

20

Ernest Hemingway's Grave

I was fly-fishing on the Big Wood River in Ketchum, Idaho, when I decided to see if I could find Ernest Hemingway's grave. The lady at the tourist center had been reluctant to give me directions, acting as if I might be a ghoul of the type she mentioned who have been chipping away chunks of tombstone for souvenirs. Her attitude almost put me off looking, but I was pretty sure I would never be in Ketchum again.

The cemetery was right on the road leading to Sun Valley. I parked on the shoulder and walked across the grass in my well-worn hip boots. A sprinkler that I failed to notice came around and ambushed me with icy droplets of water. I stood there for a short time until the sprinkler came around again.

The wire service reporter who covered the funeral got it right about the steep huge evergreen-covered mountains across the highway that leads north out of Ketchum. But he skipped – or the funeral predated – the ragtag Steinbeckian trailer park, full of T-shirted, beer-bellied men with pop tops in their fists, sitting in cheap lawn chairs and watching the tourists heading for Sun Valley, while the hip-slung women in shapeless house dresses hang out their dingy wash.

That's to the left as you stand behind the grave looking at the mountains across the highway, reading the flat headstone upside down.

"Ernest Miller Hemingway. 1898-1961."

Period, full stop.

This is where it ended.

I never read a thing that he wrote, until the year he killed himself. I strongly had disliked the macho he-man mystique that seemed to surround him in his heyday, and figured him for a buffoon.

It was a celebrated death, in a manner reserved nowadays for rock stars and Presidents. In the aftermath, the news was suddenly full of talk about his lifelong battle with depression. Then he killed himself. Even as a teenager, it was a battle that I knew intimately. The news that none of his celebrity or success had protected him made me feel badly, as if I had misjudged him.

I went straight to the Jacksonville Beach public library and checked out the only book not already loaned out, *The Old Man and the Sea*. I read it in one afternoon.

It had been my idea to force myself to read something of his as a penance for my previous harsh judgment of his life, and perhaps an act of solidarity with his depression.

But the book all by itself affected me deeply.

No one I had ever read before could write like that, putting me in the boat with Santiago as he mulled the greatness of DiMaggio and persuaded himself to fish farther and farther offshore. It was an argument I'd had with myself, and would have again, chasing ducks. I railed at Santiago, as at a live person, for not having a 12-gauge shotgun in the skiff to hold off the sharks. And I forgave his creator all his hairy-chested trespasses.

After I published my first novel at 20 and went to work for Charlie Brock on the Florida Times-Union Sunday Magazine, I discovered that Charlie was a Hemingway buff, and hewed to the macho-man image with heavy drinking, womanizing and the stated willingness to brawl with fists if the occasion warranted. Charlie had "a novel in my trunk" that he was always going to write based loosely on a story he covered in Atlanta as a UPI man. I have no idea what happened to it.

When I was drafted, Charlie thought the experience would be good for my writing. I remember him squinting at me in the bright Florida sun outside the magazine offices and predicting that I had "one or two good novels in you," if I would just get off the science fiction kick and turn to real life. It was the same thing my grandmother used to urge: "write about human emotions!" To which I would reply, smart aleck that I was, that I'd rather write about robotic emotions.

I just smiled at Charlie that day and thought he was underestimating my potential.

Now, at this grave in Idaho, I entertained the secret thought that Charlie had been overestimating. As the sprinkler came around and splashed me again, I thought that those one or two good novels Charlie predicted were one or two more than I was ever going to write. My first attempt to write about real life had left my literary agent despairing of the future, saying I wrote quite well, but "to no purpose."

Whether I ever make it or not, it all ends the same.

Famous and world-celebrated like the man whose mortal remains lay there beyond my hip boots, or footloose and full of doubt that I could even call myself a writer, it ends the same – and my constant companion, depression, never lets me forget it.

21

Visit to the City

Seattle, the corner of First and Stewart: old taverns on the corners that look just like saloons, but in 1973 the state liquor control board still absolutely forbids use of the word saloon for a drinking establishment. Fleabag hotels that gentrification has yet to touch, porn shops and a Triple-X movie theater. Beyond this claustrophobic dreariness, the eye is drawn to a broad clean vista: the ground falling away to the wide gunmetal waters of Puget Sound beneath low clouds dense with rain, stretching all the way to Bremerton. Under the clouds, the air has an absolute clarity.

Far below the taverns, a big green-and-white car ferry, etched in every detail, foams out over the wrinkled water. The blistered paint on its flanks seems starkly visible, even from this distance. Its deep, pure horn vibrates the fillings of your teeth all the way up here, cutting beneath the threshold of honky tonk and traffic noise.

Walking down past the arcades and adult bookstores in my oldest dungarees and my old Army field jacket, and a guy approaches me.

"I guess you got rid of what you were trying to sell the other day, huh?" he says to me.

Or maybe it was: "I guess you sold what you were trying to get rid of the other day, huh?"

He's as shabbily dressed as I am. Natural paranoia rears its head: I wasn't here the other day, and I don't walk the tenderloin selling things – not guns or dope or women. Am I being set up? Why? I shake my head and keep walking. He falls in.

Again: "Did you get it sold? I guess you got rid of what you were trying to sell the other day, huh?"

I shrug him off and move on.

When almost half the men you see on the street are wearing a fez, and you're not in Cairo, the Shriners are in town. In response, the street whores are out in force – twirling actual parasols, for god's sake, ankling along the street in swinging short skirts and strappy high heels, being picturesque. Just like Shirley MacLaine in that movie with Jack Lemon on the Late Show. The city sparkles with neon under the lowering sky. Sodden, dirty trash blows frenetically in the Stewart Street gutters, driven uphill by the cold wind whipping off the Sound.

I came to the city to practice to become a dirty old man, going to see *Behind the Green Door* and *Resurrection of Eve* on a double-bill. Now I will be horny on the long drive from Seattle alone in the truck, remembering other lonely horny returns from other cities that are all in the past now.

I steer along increasingly dark and deserted roads, past fields of immobile cattle and stands of dark timber, toward the glimmer of snow on the foothills; driving deeper and deeper into that remote and always mysterious rural fastness that I now am calling home.

22

Richard Brautigan's Cowboy Boots

So I wound up marrying a girl from the Pacific Northwest whose dad was a Norwegian with the wanderlust. His wanderings ended abruptly beneath the fall of a massive Douglas fir when he didn't hear the faller's warning above the racket of the noisy chain saws that were replacing misery whips and double-bitted axes in the 1950s.

She was eight that year, and somehow took it into her head that if she was a good enough little girl, her father would return to her. That was one of the saddest things I ever heard.

Daughter of a wanderer, she drifted with me during my newspaper gypsy days. We came home to the Northwest the year after her mother died. It was the same year her oldest sister came home from Norway, leaving a marriage to her Norwegian first cousin during which they had lived on the same land their family had occupied on the heights above Bergen for four hundred years.

I began to learn things about the Norse: each generation seemed to spin off at least one wanderer like

my wife's father, who settled far away, while the rest
stayed close to the ancestral land. The stay-at-homes liked
to travel, too; they thought nothing of visiting across the
planet to far-flung descendants of the wanderers, before
returning to the Land of the Midnight Sun. Children of the
wanderers routinely made pilgrimages to the home
country. To the offspring of Vikings, it seemed, the whole
wide world was a smallish neighborhood.

There seemed a special affinity between the Pacific
Northwest and the Norse. Not only family members from
Norway, but family acquaintances, would show up for
visits. That's how I encountered Richard Brautigan's
cowboy boots.

Brautigan was an American writer of unusual gifts
who enjoyed a vogue in that strange time in America that
bridged the era of the Beat Generation and that of the
hippies with flowers in their hair. He spent a lot of time in
San Francisco with the hippies, but he was a Pacific
Northwest native.

"I was about 17," Brautigan wrote about his arrival in
California and living in a pasteboard-lined shack across
from a welfare mom, "and made lonely and strange by that
Pacific Northwest of so many years ago, that dark, rainy
land..."

I would never have known a thing about his work if I
hadn't married into the Northwest. Brautigan's words had
come to represent the drowned landscape of Western
Washington as surely as the coming and going of the
traveling Norwegians.

I was reading his unusual prose when the Norwegian
poet came visiting in 1973. I never quite grasped the poet's

connection to my in-laws; he didn't have a lot of English and the in-laws took his arrival as a matter of course without need of explanation.

So there he stood in our foyer, long and lanky and with limp blond locks over his shirt collar, because part of visiting was to stop in at every house connected to his host.

A Norwegian poet wearing cowboy boots. I wondered if he was a Wild West fan.

But no, he had received the boots as a gift from Richard Brautigan when he visited the writer in San Francisco on his way to the Northwest. I heard "Brautigan" amid the Norwegian consonants. His hostess and translator, my sister-in-law, explained that Brautigan was quite popular in Norway.

The lanky poet's smile was as wide as the Midnight Sun; on his pilgrimage to San Francisco, his icon had given him his cowboy boots! Not only that, Brautigan had personally described the Pacific Northwest to him. I thought about one of the author's descriptions in the book I was reading then:

"... the Pacific Northwest: a haunted land where nature dances the minuet with people and danced with me in those old bygone days..."

The Norse poet had been completely dazzled by his meeting with the author; that needed no translation. Now, wearing Brautigan's cowboy boots, he seemed ready to step out right this minute in a haunted quadrille.

Then he was gone, to continue his rambles in Richard Brautigan's boots until the fjords called him home.

23

Arkansas Toothpick

My poor bantam rooster of a father; ancient black and white prewar photographs show him slim and smiling beside my radiant mother holding a bundled baby blanket that had me inside, neat enough in his uniform to stand inspection on our front porch. The unerringly truthful eye of the Kodak reveals that he stood exactly as tall as she did.

No two ways about it, he was a little man.

In a lifetime's reflection upon the man who fathered me I have concluded that all he was and ever would be was constrained and shaped by his short stature.

He was the youngest of a large spread of siblings fathered by an Arkansas blacksmith of legendary strength (they said he could throw a baseball through a board fence) and a sturdy wife who could have been part Apache or perhaps Comanche. You didn't ask about half-breeds in the hearing of the blacksmith, not if you wanted to avoid broken body parts. But it was as if the robust genes of his parents had exhausted themselves with his older, stronger, larger siblings, and my father was all they had left to give.

I suppose it is no wonder he felt comfortable among my tall maternal uncles, one of whom had introduced him to my mother after a downtown military parade. They probably treated him like a mascot, pretty much the same way his father and older siblings had treated him in Arkansas. He was certainly accustomed to being the smallest weakest one, though he could spin a good tale at a campfire and liked to make up blustering stories about how he beat up larger men in Army fistfights. My uncles tended to punch holes in his bombast. Here's a story I heard many times:

"So I hauled off and hit that drunken sumbich right in the ear and he..."

"Well, Bill – anybody can beat up a drunk."

"Well – he wasn't drunk."

"But you said he was drunk."

"Well he'd been drinking. But he was *big.*"

And then everybody would laugh while he fumed.

Little-man syndrome; the large genes skipped him entirely and came to rest in me, from both sides of my family tree. When you stand inches north of six feet and weigh thirty to fifty pounds above 200, you find that you don't like aggressive little men who yip at you like Pekinese. Long ago, a seasoned battler told me that if a small man attacks you, you always lose: if you swat him down, you're a bully and if he somehow scores a lucky punch, he's a hero. Truer advice was never spoken.

Fortunately I was far too young to know these things before he went off to war, and my earliest memories of him were happy ones. When the family gathered devotedly before the giant walnut console of the living-room radio to listen the Grand Ole Opry, I would rush in from wherever I was playing and shout "Bill sings! Bill sings!"

It wasn't my father, of course. It was Ernest Tubbs. But in my young memory my father was always singing lonesome hillbilly songs when he wasn't playing his "mouth harp" with piercing beauty. The young women of my hometown liked him a lot – small dapper men always seem to have that effect on women, I have noticed over the years. My mother's best girlfriend said that when he walked down the street, women said "yum-yum."

He even impressed my grandmother, who lived by a tough code of behavior. She said that my father was "the sweetest of them all," high praise indeed when you knew how much she loved her own sons.

I was born into war. My first sense memory is the smell of duffel bags in the front hall, and the coming and going of khaki giants who always seemed to be laughing. They tossed me high in the air toward the remote ceiling until I laughed so hard I thought I would bust. Then came the long silent time when all the giants picked up their duffel bags and went away to war. My next vivid memories are of cold and bitter winters between the humid summers, when I had to be cautioned repeatedly about sneaking too close to the coal fires burning red-hot in open fireplace grates. The smell of burning coal meant home forevermore, and years later the smell of coal fires in Cold War Germany snatched me back in memory to the fireplaces of home as fast as a dog snaps at a fly.

Germany was where my uncles and father went when I was still learning to walk, leaving my fireman grandfather the only grown man in the house. During the long absence of the khaki giants, my mother was the only one who smelled like duffel bags, because she stitched canvas

99

covers for tanks and artillery at the arsenal on the hill.

When the khaki giants came home, they didn't laugh all the time anymore. My father didn't play his harmonica in the house anymore. It was years before I learned that was because the playing reminded him too much of lost comrades who had called out requests from adjacent foxholes.

I was entranced by the war booty they brought home for me to play with: JugendKorps daggers and red Nazi armbands and Wehrmacht helmets, and those funny-shaped canteens, and a tiny camp stove fueled with alcohol. They brought German precision binoculars for my grandfather, and my infantry uncle never forgave the sergeant who hijacked his boxful of captured Mauser rifles, with which he had intended to arm the whole clan for deer hunting in the Georgia swamps.

My uncles no longer thought of my father as a kind of mascot.

But their changed view was not out of respect because he had waded ashore at Normandy with the rest of the Fourth Division and fought all the way to Germany. They held him in contempt.

Because, right after he got home, they caught him cheating on their sister. It was only a small town, and everybody knew each other's business, and he had very little chance of getting away with it under those circumstances, but he did it anyway.

I would have no idea of the full enormity of his transgression until I was more than fifty years old.

But little pitchers have big ears, so I knew something awful had happened. My staff-officer uncle had confronted him with the evidence of his cheating and then stepped aside for my infantry uncle to beat the living crap out of him.

He had pulled a knife. A real Arkansas toothpick, whatever that was.

My maternal grandfather walked into the room.

Ah, my grandfather – the stories they told in that small river city about him! The one the townspeople loved was about an armed gangster in a barbershop, back in Prohibition, bragging harshly about what he would do to my grandfather for marrying the bootlegger chieftain's girlfriend. The neighboring barber then whipped away the hot towels masking the face of the customer he was pampering, and my grandfather sat up blinking from his nap.

The armed bootlegger – his pistol in plain view in his shoulder holster with his coat laid aside for a trim and a facial – fainted.

Just fainted, dead away, right there in the barber chair.

"What the hell's wrong with him?" my grandfather grumbled – and they said you could hear the barbers' laughter all the way down the street to Fire Department Headquarters. The whole town liked to tell tall tales about the fright with which otherwise-tough men confronted the ferocious force of nature that was my grandfather.

Now, with my father having drawn a knife on my uncles, my grandfather sneered at this sinister Arkansas toothpick (whatever that was) and told him that he would shove it up his ass and leave it there if he ever saw his face again.

My father didn't faint. He ran.

Literally ran – down the front hall where I first smelled duffel bags, out the heavy front door with its stained-glass panels set in wrought iron framing the main frosted glass, and away. He stayed gone for a long time.

But that didn't stop the family from talking about him. He was the one person, other than me, for which my grandmother always made allowances in her iron code of conduct. But she was deeply disappointed at his behavior. Not the cheating so much – men would be men, in her jaundiced view – but the knife was out of bounds, an admission of his little-man syndrome that she equated to cowardice, no matter how much combat he had seen. For anyone else, that judgment would have been the kiss of death in her regard for him. But she had a soft spot for him, and decided generously that the war had proved too heavy for his sensitive nature, crushing out all his native sweetness, leaving only a frightened little man.

Others disagreed. My uncles, spreading the story of his cheating and his cowardice abroad, began to pick up stories from other soldiers who had served in peacetime camps with him before the war. This little pitcher hung near the doors of rooms where the adults talked softly about such things, and got a big earful. My father won those fights he always bragged about with a knife, something he had never seen fit to mention. He never cut anyone fatally, so since they were going to war anyway, the Army let it go and he avoided stockade time. Just like he had avoided jail as a teenager when he stole a neighbor's car and the Arkansas judge permitted him to enlist rather than go to jail.

I learned much later that my maternal grandfather never understood the Army's – or my grandmother's – leniency toward my father. He had served as an able-bodied seaman in the days of coal-burning battleships before the First World War, but was "sent out," in the terse words of his seaman's diary, on a BCD when he smashed a swaggering Chief Petty Officer to pulp with his bare hands for calling him a nigger.

Stealing a workingman's Model T or using a knife in fistfights were dishonorable things by my grandfather's lights. Workers in the cotton mills, where he labored before he got on with the fire department, fought to bloody, exhausted draws without ever resorting to the razor-sharp bobbin knives on their belts. But my father had escaped the consequences of his dishonorable behavior, while my grandfather had been punished by the Navy for defending the purity of his blood with his fists.

(A kind of purity; city legend whispered that when he was just a boy about my age, and his clan came down out of North Carolina, migrating ahead of trouble with the law to do with moonshine stills, there hadn't been much doubt that they were half-blood Cherokees whose roots traced back to the mountain renegades who refused to walk Andrew Jackson's Trail of Tears and clung to their hidden hollows with the tenacity exhibited much later by the bronco Apaches of the Southwest. But that's another story.)

Young memory doesn't mark the years by calendar. I was three when I ran to hear Bill sing on the Grand Ole Opry before he came home. I was almost four when he went away again. My mother remarried, this time to a childhood sweetheart who'd had his own bad war in the Pacific, and come home bald as a billiard. Nobody spoke much any more about my vanished father.

The next thing I knew, I was six years old, in first grade, and two giant city detectives were sitting in the principal's office waiting for me when my teacher brought me to them. The little pitcher with the big ears waited outside the door while they told the teacher why they were there, and cautioned her: "Don't let him hear that his daddy is back around with that big knife of his, threatening to cut off his head. But keep your eye out."

There were other words – I recall "blood-crazy GI" – before the two giants squeezed me between them in the front seat of a black '49 Ford and drove me the four blocks home. My grandfather, in his dress fireman's blues, was waiting at the house, called home from Old Number One. My two maternal uncles still in town – the staff officer had moved on to the Pentagon – showed up soon after.

"I warned that son of a bitch," my grandfather said coldly.

The cops of course all knew him – everybody did. Then too, his brother-in-law, one of my grandmother's seven brothers, was head of the Vice Squad. They told him they would take care of it.

"Not if I see him first," he said. They didn't argue – nobody in that town argued with my grandfather.

My grandmother and mother hustled me into the kitchen and got me settled with a frosty bottle of Coca Cola. I could hear my grandfather thumping around in his bedroom off the kitchen. He came out wearing work clothes and a lightweight jacket. My youngest uncle stayed behind with the family shotgun while the other two went on the prowl.

They never found my father. He was gone again.

But he came back again, and then again. Each time he was spotted, city detectives took me home from school. The cops and my family hunted for him each time, but they never caught up with him. He kept popping into the area, repeating his threats to cut off my head, but he had the little man's gift of vanishing again before the hunters showed up. My mother sneered and said she'd break his damn neck herself if he showed up at the house.

Even now, decades later, it is difficult to recall the emotional storms I went through. I was horribly embarrassed, mainly, for being hauled out of class so many times to be taken home by cops. I knew all about heads being cut off, because I read my uncle's pulp war magazines about the war in the Pacific and Japanese officers with their wicked curved swords who decapitated helpless GIs. I suppose I must have been afraid, but maybe not. I may have wondered what I was guilty of, for my father to hate me so, since children tend to blame themselves for things. But I don't remember any of that. The furious contempt with which the skulking little man was viewed by the people I knew best seemed to rub off on me.

Amazingly, my grandmother still took his side. He was just too soft for that kind of war, she would tell me when no one else was around, and it broke him, broke something inside him. Try not to hate him too much. Of course he's not going to cut off your head. He's just talking big because he's such a little man full of such big pain. I listened – nobody *didn't* listen to my grandmother's pronouncements – but I think I was developing my own ideas about little men and cowards.

Looking back from the long perspective of six decades, it was probably about then that I started having the sleep problems that dogged my entire life. I would lie awake, watching and waiting, listening to the family sleep, staring out the night windows as far as I could see, waiting for the first lurching step of The Thing or the Creature from the Black Lagoon, coming to get me before the family could wake up.

A shrink told me in my fifties that my fear of the horror movies that were quite the vogue those years, and that I hated with a passion, was probably displacement: the real monster was my elusive knife-wielding father. I don't know about that. I do know that it was not unusual to stay awake until dawn's early light, and then, having survived the dangerous night, fall asleep. I was tired all the time during the day.

The only time I could sleep normally was when we went to the beach for vacation; I reasoned that the monsters wouldn't know to look for me there, and the sound of the surf was somehow reassuring.

The sightings of my father stopped sometime before my grandfather retired and we all moved – my grandparents, my twice-divorced mother, my younger brother and me – to a house two doors from the ocean in Florida. Night terrors faded from my memory. I always trusted the sea, even when it stood up and roared under the lash of hurricanes; that was an honest kind of fury that I could understand and even admire. The years stacked up and suddenly I was on the verge of graduating from high school.

I was shocked beyond words when my mother took me aside one morning before breakfast and asked if I'd like to meet my father again, because he was right here, on the beaches where we lived now. He had called from a fancy motel on Jacksonville Beach, on vacation with his second wife and son, who wanted to meet his older brother.

My shock turned to inarticulate rage; I felt betrayed by my closest family. My mother seemed excited at the idea of seeing him, and my grandmother said with some satisfaction that it sounded as if he had got on with his life. Wasn't I curious at all?

All the bad emotions came roaring out of hiding as if they had never been away. How could they even countenance contact with the evil little man? In the face of their inexplicable about-face, I was essentially speechless. But I could and did say "No!" loudly and repeatedly. And breathed a huge sigh of relief when they honored my wishes. The little band of aliens decamped Florida that same day to return to Kentucky, where my mother said he was living now.

Strange how vividly those bygone days are carved into my memory.

More than strange.

Over half a century has passed since that Florida morning, when my father came out of nowhere to haunt me again, and it was my turn to chase him away.

Because in real life, unlike movies, there never seems to be a fade to black until every last survivor is buried.

I don't remember when my mother admitted to me

that she was staying in telephone contact with my father – but I know she had to build me up for the news that he was fixing up a car for me at his automotive shop in Kentucky, at her request. There of course had never been a dime of support from him over the years, and she said now he wanted to make some of that up to me. I had my first full-time job and needed a car to drive to the city every day, but I had no faith that the evil little man would come through, or had a conscience, despite my grandmother's beliefs. I was very young and cynical, and I could see clearly that there was a lot more in play than just him fixing up a car for me.

My suspicions bore out when I was informed that the entire bunch of us – my grandparents, my mother, my brother, me – were invited to meet him in Atlanta to take delivery on my car. We were to meet him alone, no son to hide behind as his reason for making contact, and certainly no second wife to cramp his style. He would fly home after I got my car.

We stayed at a fancy motel called the Georgian Oaks – all on his tab. He had reinvented himself all right – as a successful businessman, inventor of tools for disassembly of automatic transmissions, high-ranking Mason. The slim soldier was long gone, replaced by a stocky little man in tailored business suits with shoes so highly shined his old sergeants would have approved. Somewhere along the line, he'd lost the little finger of his right hand working on car engines.

I waited with bated breath as we pulled into the Georgian Oaks parking lot. My grandfather, driving his big '55 Mercury as deftly as he ever handled those big

LaFrance trucks out of Old Number One, braked to a stop and stepped out to face my father, waiting outside the office. I don't know what kind of fireworks I expected, but I expected something.

My grandfather nodded once, like a hatchet falling, and my father's trademark grin from those faded pre-war photos emerged from the fleshiness of his older face.

They shook hands.

They shook hands.

Without fanfare or ceremony, as casually as if they'd seen each other a week ago, and in unstressed circumstances.

My mother got out of the car and hugged him, and my grandmother patted him on the back and smiled fondly. Then it was my turn to shake hands – that's when I noticed the missing digit, and how he used the remainder of his fingers like a crab claw to exert tremendous force. I rode it out grimly without crushing his knuckles together, but I can't say I wasn't tempted. But he let go quickly enough, with a nervous little laugh. "Big hands," he said.

Somehow we got registered and into the restaurant where he had reserved a table for lunch. He had already been there long enough to have the waitresses all a-flutter around him, as if he was some well-liked big shot. The very ordinariness of the table conversation was beyond my grasp. The weight of things unspoken seemed almost suffocating, and then merely banal – this was the way grownups conducted their business, apparently.

The rest of the visit went on pretty much in that same vein. He took my brother and me for a ride in my new car, a pristine '52 Chevrolet. We went to visit a guy who was building the tools he had invented and listened to them discuss getting them into a mechanic's catalog. He noticed that Earl was kind of hanging back, and commented that he wasn't getting much attention this trip – what he needed was some spending money to enjoy himself – so he slipped him a twenty. My brother seemed to think my father was pretty cool after that, certainly nothing like the tight-fisted miser his father was.

Only one image from that trip is burned into my brain.

I barged into our room unexpectedly and caught my mother and father in a passionate embrace – and saw him bounce out of her arms and halfway across the room looking like a guilty schoolboy. My mother was smirking; I had the unworthy thought, as I about-faced and left, that she was enjoying being the other woman this time around.

Of course my grandmother had a different take when I told her: that they had only truly ever loved each other, and it was a damned shame how things had got messed up back when I was a toddler, because look how nicely he'd turned out.

So the years rolled on. I categorically refuse to say that he became "a part of my life." But he was always in the background after that. When my car blew its head gasket, he reached out long distance to a fellow member of the Independent Garage Owners association, and had it fixed good as new. When the first transmission fell out of it, he shipped a new one to Florida and came after it to personally supervise its installation. And, of course, to spend a couple days, off the books of his present life, with my mother.

I had some successes of my own, got drafted, smelled

coal smoke in postwar Germany, discovered women for myself, had contretemps behind that, got married. He invited me north to introduce my wife to his second wife and my other brother, who it turned out really had always wanted to meet his older sibling. The visit was nice, but I could not help feeling like a traitor sitting at the breakfast table of my stepmother, watching his interactions with her and comparing them unfavorably to his happy-go-lucky ways around my mother. I had become one of those grownups full of unspoken things just beneath the polite table conversation and I didn't like it all that much.

The years continued their relentless march. My stepmother was afflicted with Alzheimer's disease not long after my maternal grandmother was. My father broke his fragile health trying to care for her – because my mother had kept my grandmother in her house until the bitter end, and he wanted to prove that he was as strong as she was. It didn't make a lot of sense to me, but there it was. My mother didn't survive my grandmother by much – cancer took her, and she came to live with my family until the end, refusing treatment to spend time with her grandchildren. She couldn't bear to tell my father or her surviving brothers that she was dying – she left that assignment to me.

After that had run its course, I found myself making more trips to Kentucky to try to shore up my father through his myriad surgeries. My younger brother – his other son – had died in a car crash, and my stepmother went into deep mourning that morphed into Alzheimer's. I wound up sleeping in his room down the hall from my father, and when my typical fragmented sleep would drive me out into the hall, I would instantly hear his voice, low and urgent: "Is everything okay?"

It turned out that I was not the only one who slept poorly all those years. The older he got, the more fragile, the more his combat memories rose to haunt his nights. The worst memory, the one that invaded his dreams most often, was of a night spent sleeping in a snowy foxhole on the edge of Germany, one of a picket line of seven fox holes, and awakening to discover that Germans had been in the lines that night with knives, and cut six throats before stopping short of his position for reasons known but to God.

He liked to go driving in the night to settle his nerves – and by then I was doing the driving because he couldn't quite stay between the lines anymore. We'd stop at some diner for a snack and he would ramble off into tales of his life, almost talking to himself. I was no longer the little pitcher with the big ears, I was the big man going gray himself, with hearing losses attributable to various rough experiences of my own. Sometimes I didn't think he knew quite who I was – I was almost an exact clone of one of his older brothers, Henry, in size and comportment, and sometimes I think he was telling Henry his tales instead of me. He mumbled quite a bit after his stroke.

But I clearly heard the words that one night in a steak shack, because the background music had stilled for the evening. The words that finally described the enormity of his infidelity that had cost him the marriage to my mother all those weary years ago.

I think it fair to say my back hairs stood up, because there was no slightest trace of regret, of stricken conscience, or even an awareness of to whom he told the story across the remnants of the steaks.

"My buddy was still in the hospital in England," he said with that old up-from-under grin that had charmed so many women across the years. "He asked me to take care of his wife until he could get home." He kind of chuckled under his breath. "I took care of her all right, she couldn't get enough of the way I took care of her. The way she kept bragging to her mother, I thought I was going to have to do her mother, too." He chuckled again and fiddled with his coffee cup. "Well, then I had to leave town kind of sudden. She wanted me to send her a bus ticket to come wherever I ended up. I told her I would. But I never did."

So there it was – the enormity of the act by the little man my grandmother said was the sweetest of them all: cheating on my mother with the wife of his wounded comrade, and then abandoning her into the bargain. You couldn't call it a final confession, not told with that snigger.

He died on Valentine's Day, the year before the Twin Towers fell. He left his estate in such a mess that it took years to untangle, and the looters and the lawyers got most of it.

But tucked among my souvenirs is that notorious Arkansas Toothpick, hand-crafted for him by a cousin on his father's blacksmith forge in Arkansas – as slim and deadly as that slim simpering soldier in those old photographs, holding a baby blanket with the infant bundled inside that he later threatened with the knife.

My father's war knife mine now,
willed to me when he died

– – – – – – – – – – – – – – – – – – – –

Hand-built custom blade
His cousin smithed it well
fits my hand quite well

In endless sleepless foxholes
that knife lay beneath his hand

– -

He built a new life
after his philandering
put his blade away

we met when I was a teen
my grandfather shook his hand

– – – – – – – – – – – – – – – – – – – –

Dapper little man
I had expected fireworks
They smiled, shook hands

muscular retired fireman
and a blacksmith's bantam son

– – – – – – – – – – – – – – – –

Fickle irony

asleep in my father's house
jerking myself awake

soft voice: Did you hear something?
fearful, from my father's room

– – – – – – – – – – – – – – – – – – – -

Shadows haunted him,
long-dead buddies and Germans,
into his late seventies

A sleepless master bedroom
like a foxhole lost in time

– – – – – – – – – – – – – – – – – – – -

He said only this:
that foxhole nights fought with knives
were worse than gunfire

Worst night of all, he lived,
six buddies died in grim silence

– – – – – – – – – – – – – – – – – – – –

Sweetest of them all
my grandmother said of him
war used him all up

Foxholes held him in his mind
a captive until he died

— — — — — — — — — — — — — — — — — —
Obituary:
He succeeded in his life
worked hard, made money

Drove a classic Cadillac
built a business from scratch
— — — — — — — — — — —
Nothing in the news
about stalking his first son
with a combat knife

It sleeps in my souvenirs
a long way from Arkansas

24

Best Shot I Ever Made

Best shot I ever made.

Absolutely without question the best shot I ever made.

And the last shot I ever fired in Arizona.

I was giving up one of the best jobs I ever had, publications editor for the Arizona Game and Fish Department, with some of the best people I ever knew. I was moving back to Washington State to work as a bureaucrat in an unpopular state agency that I knew next to nothing about.

Before I made that shot, my mother's boyfriend had quizzed me about my decision:

"You have here a job where you can go hunting and fishing as part of your work-day, right? Travel all over the state, building up a lot of comp time?" Danny said.

Yep.

"Then when you get back from the field, you can put in for comp time for the work time you spent fishing and hunting – so that you can go fishing or hunting on your own. Right?"

Yep.

"And yet you're leaving to go wear a suit and tie and sit in an office," Danny said. "You must be crazy."

I admit he gave me second thoughts. But we had two small children that we didn't want to see grow up in a city the size of Phoenix, and none of us liked the desert. I could reassign myself to the mountains when it got intolerable, but the wife and kids could not.

So we sold our Arizona house – within a half-hour after we put out the for-sale sign. It was that kind of market in Phoenix in the late 1970s. The new buyers almost trampled us in the doorway, moving their stuff in before we could get fully vacated. We checked into a motel to sort ourselves out from that craziness. While the wife and the kids enjoyed the pool, I took the dogs out west of the Black Canyon Shooting Range because the dove season had just started and it seemed the right way to say farewell to the desert.

And I made the best shot of my life.

Harry the Dog was my first Labrador, and my best pal. I had acquired Paka, a half-golden, to give him a mate. Pirate was my pick from their second litter that I hoped to be Harry's heir. Poor old Pirate, a hard-luck pup almost from birth.

A black Labrador born in Arizona; a winter dog where summer ruled. He was the sweetest-natured of the pups; a little shy, a little goofy. As a puppy he learned quickly that he fell at the bottom of the pack structure beneath his dad and then his mom. If he could have talked, he might have called that bad luck too, not to have a family all to himself, as all the litter mates that we sold did.

Snake-bit as a term has come to mean hard luck.

Poor old Pirate had his share of hard luck his whole too-short life. But I console myself with the memory that when he was six months old and almost got snake-bit for real, I made the best shot of my life.

The dogs panted heavily the September heat. Harry sneezed incessantly in the dust, trying to pick up the trail of a mourner I winged early. Paka gave up trying and came to heel. Pirate romped with the exuberance of puppy-hood, poking his nose into everything. An errant worry crossed my mind for a moment. But then here came reliable Harry trotting, the dove precisely and gently centered beneath his graying muzzle.

Paka swiped it right out of his mouth. Harry was so soft-mouthed he would never clamp down and fight for possession. Paka mouthed the bird and dropped it, spitting out pinfeathers. Pirate pranced in, scooped in up and delivered it to hand. I was so proud of him. I consoled Harry about Paka's bad behavior and grumbled at her.

When I looked up, Pirate had wandered off to my left, busily nosing the base of a majestic saguaro cactus to see if he could find something else to bring me.

I heard him yelp. I caught a peripheral glimpse of him springing backwards on stiff legs...

The rest is etched in my brain.

The rattler was already in mid-strike, uncoiling, sunlight flashing off its scales, launching at Pirate's throat. Pirate's lunge had not carried him beyond reach.

My Browning went off.

A tight burst of dust exploded between the snake and the dog.

I have no memory of aiming, or releasing the safety, or firing. John M. Browning's Automatic Five, the legendary humpbacked autoloader, was my favorite shotgun; it had fit me the first day I picked it up as if tailor-made. It earned its keep that last day in Arizona.

The long sinewy length of reptile thrashed convulsively, beating up a hanging cloud of dust. Pirate stood rooted, trembling, ears at half-mast, cowering as if he had done something bad. I approached cautiously in the face of that reptilian thrashing, gun still shouldered.

The snake's head was gone. Just gone.

Its gore damped some of the dust stirred by the body's throes. At that range, the load of Number 9 shot couldn't have been much bigger than my fist.

I examined Pirate carefully, gentling his tremors. I was afraid I'd find pellet wounds. I didn't. Then I searched carefully through his dense neck fur for fang punctures.

My logical brain told me that it is impossible to outdraw a rattlesnake that has already launched. But my mind's eye replayed the sequence: I saw the snake in mid-strike – the gun went off. The actions seemed simultaneous.

The rattler had been coiled in deep shadow at the base of the saguaro. The flash of its moving body in the sun when it went after Pirate must have triggered my neural fire control array. The result was beyond reason.

But the snake was dead. Pirate was untouched.

I noticed a faint after-tremor in my hands. The day was heating up. Doves still were flitting above a dry watercourse among the crowns of mesquite trees. But there was no way I could top that shot. I headed back to the truck with the mature dogs contentedly at heel. They both probably had visions of the big canteen and the hubcap drinking dish back at the truck. Pirate, puppy spirits recovered, was exploring again, perhaps a little more carefully.

When I dropped the tailgate and got out the hubcap, he was gone again.

I watered the adult dogs, kenneled Paka and sent Harry along our back trail to find his wayward offspring. We were halfway back to the dry wash where I killed the snake when the most heart-rending howl I'd ever heard came wavering mournfully through the heat mirage. My immediate horrified thought was that I had missed puncture wounds, and the pup was dying.

But no, Pirate was sitting in a clearing, nose pointed soulfully at the blazing sky – and a wicked cholla cactus was imbedded in his forepaw. I sighed and dug my pliers out of my old shooting vest. Snake-bit in every sense of the word – except the original. That was our dog, Pirate.

Thanks to the best shot I ever made in my life.

25

Brautigan's Unlucky .44

It came to pass that I spent most of the first decade of the twenty-first century in the company of a little red-headed girl who was one of the smartest people I ever knew, with catholic, small "c" tastes in literature. Though she had spent years studying the most obfuscatory philosophical texts, and affected an annoying superiority about them, she had an instant response for me the day I told her my chocolate Labrador retriever's name was McGee.

"For Travis McGee," she said promptly. "The *Busted Flush,* Slip F-18, Bahia Mar. Fort Lauderdamndale."

We had a complex and complicated relationship that was never boring, and sometimes she exhibited insights so swift and deep they left me stunned.

One day I was ruminating over the suicides of two writers for whom I always had a particular affinity: Ernest Hemingway and Richard Brautigan. I once had made a pilgrimage to Hemingway's Idaho gravesite in search of insights of my own. I well remembered a phrase of his about his own father's suicide: that he had "misused" the gun.

Being me, I wondered why Hemingway had chosen the particular shotgun that he had that fateful morning. It had been variously reported as his favorite, and identified at least once as a Boss. If the latter, the contemporary iterations of the brand were breath-takingly expensive; you could buy a lot of houses for less. If the Boss, had there been any unconscious economic message in the selection, born of his years of fiscal struggles? According to one of his Idaho hunting buddies of the happy days there, his favorite duck gun had been a Browning Superposed that he won at a shoot overseas. Had some final fondness for that piece kept him from selecting it for his own misuse? Unknowable, and who but me would even wonder?

The only time that I could remember seriously considering such misuse of a firearm, the one that came most readily to hand was a scaled-down Colt single-action revolver, a .22. It was the only pistol I owned then. My police-reporting days had taught that a .22 slug will often rattle around inside the brainpan and do every bit as much lethal damage as a larger round. Such an image was, ultimately, disgusting and off-putting, and I put away such thoughts.

Which led me, the way my mind works, to the .44 Magnum revolver that Richard Brautigan had borrowed to finish his existence. I set aside the selfishness that such an act implied: the guilt that he would lay on the loaning friend. Suicide after all is the utmost act of selfishness, however warranted it may seem to the doer.

I was reading a much-folded newspaper clipping about

how Brautigan had died, and pondering. My little redheaded girl noticed my brown study and inquired.

"Richard Brautigan," I said. "Why a .44 Magnum? It seems so out of character with the gentleness of his writing."

"Brautigan is so intimately linked to San Francisco," she said immediately. "He wasn't feeling lucky that day."

"What?"

"The other San Francisco icon is Dirty Harry," she said, with just a trace of impatience.

"Oh," I said.

26

99-cent Vacation in Paris

On the far downside of sixty, the only thing that resembles a television set in my small cluttered low-income apartment is a portable videotape monitor. I used it twenty years ago when I was writing television spots and didn't have the heart just to trash it when I closed out my storage unit. I had some vague notion of showing old VHS copies of some spots for which I won awards back then to – well, I didn't know to whom. Who would care? But anyway I kept it. Not long thereafter, when I stopped at the local Goodwill Store to pick up a couple of used books, I was surprised to see stacks of VHS movies near the book shelves: dozens and dozens of them, some still pristine in their original shrink wrap.

The price was 99 cents apiece.

Labels and stickers on the boxes identified once-prosperous video rental stores, as well as grocery chains. The clerk said they were either donated as surplus or collected when stores went out of business.

A relentless flood of technology has inundated many of my favorite things: my old manual typewriters, then my stacking record player, then the eight-track tape player in my '71 VW Beetle and finally dash radios with readable dials and a tuning knob with which to chase the atmospheric skip across a darkened nation.

Here at last, in a Goodwill store in Washington State, the tide had washed up technological flotsam perfect for my old monitor.

I couldn't have been more tickled if I'd stumbled across a functioning record player for my old long-playing records that haven't been out of their sheaths for thirty years. I grabbed *Patton, Field of Dreams, The Thirteenth Warrior, Basic Instinct* and a few so forgettable that I tossed them only half played. I seemed to be the only one buying them.

In all my years of living with sleep apnea, I have never figured out how to wear reading glasses with my CPAP mask. Reading myself to sleep hasn't been an option in decades. My vision is fine, unaided, across the room, so the 99-cent specials became my go-to-sleep entertainment. Sometimes the plots got all tangled up in my dreams, not a bad thing if the movie featured Sharon Stone, for instance.

This is all preamble to my discovery of a concert video of Diana Krall in Paris.

Diana Krall is a bluesy blonde of whom I had never heard, with incredibly nimble fingers on a piano keyboard and a strong, unusual voice. She was sided by very talented drums and strings, and backed up by something approaching a full orchestra that happened to be salted with a lot of good-looking women that I could well imagine tripping lightly down the Paris boulevards past the sidewalk cafes that I knew as a young soldier.

Diana Krall's raw, slangy delivery sang me to sleep the first night. Once her sideman's electric-guitar solo took me away, and another time the solitary thudding of the superb base player. The mellow smoothness of the supporting orchestra was almost subliminal. And boy! Can she tickle those ivories!

The high tide of technology rolls ever onward, leaving me happily marooned back here, smiling in the dark with Diana Krall on my 99-cent vacation in Paris.

Thank you for reading.
Please review this book. Reviews help others find
Absolutely Amazing eBooks and inspire us to keep
providing these marvelous tales.

If you would like to be put on our email list to receive
updates on new releases, contests, and promotions, please
go to AbsolutelyAmazingEbooks.com and sign up.

Bonus

By going to The New Atlantian Library website (NewAtlantianLibrary.com) and entering the password below into the Bonus Reward Section, you can read a another short story by William R. Burkett, Jr. – for **free!**

AA1027

About the Author

William R. Burkett, Jr. is an acclaimed sci-fi writer, listed in the *Science Fiction Encyclopedia*. But his "straight" writing is a well-kept secret, until now. A product of Georgia and Florida, he now lives in the Pacific Northwest where he can enjoy the fishing and duck hunting. He was once described by author Frank G. Slaughter as a "natural-born storyteller." After a Quixotic career in journalism and public relations, he's now turning his attention back to his trusty typewriter, uh, we mean computer. "Times change, but good storytelling goes on forever," he says.

The New
Atlantian Library

NewAtlantianLibrary.com
or AbsolutelyAmazingeBooks.com
or AA-eBooks.com

www.ingramcontent.com/pod-product-compliance
Lightning Source LLC
Chambersburg PA
CBHW050410030726
47503CB00006B/2122